SLEEPING JENNY

Part One of
the Timesurfers

Aubrie Dionne

SPENCER
HILL
PRESS

Spencer Hill Press

This book is a work of fiction. Names, characters, places, and
incidents are products of the author's imagination or are used
fictitiously. Any resemblance to actual events, locales, or persons,
living or dead, is entirely coincidental.

Contact: Spencer Hill Press, PO Box 247,
Contoocook, NH 03229, USA

Please visit our website at www.spencerhillpress.com

First Edition: December 2014
Aubrie Dionne
Sleeping Jenny/by Aubrie Dionne–1st ed.
p. cm.

Summary:
After being frozen for three hundred years in hopes of a cure
for her cancer, a teenage girl struggles to find her place in a future
without the animals she loves so dearly.

The author acknowledges the copyrighted or trademarked status
and trademark owners of the following wordmarks mentioned in
this fiction: Abercrombie, American Idol, Barbie, Baywatch, Beverly
Hills 90210, Boeing, Buffy the Vampire Slayer, Buzz Lightyear,
Cheshire Cat, Chevy, Disney/Disney's Animal Kingdom, CSI,
Dunkin' Donuts, Elmo, ESPN, Expedition Everest, Gossip Girl,
Hummer, iPhone, Jeep, Jetsons, Ken doll, Kindle, Lexus, Miss
Universe, Mountain Dew, National Geographic, NBC, Peter Pan,
Smurfs, SpongeBob SquarePants, Star Trek, Taylor Swift, The
Twilight Zone, Transformers, Velcro, Welch's, Wicked Witch of the
West, YMCA

Cover design by Kate Kaynak
Interior layout by Errick A. Nunnally

978-1-939392-39-8 (paperback)
978-1-939392-40-4 (e-book)

Printed in the United States of America

To everyone who follows dreams. Persist and persevere.

CHAPTER ONE

Neverland

"**W**hat if I wake up after World War IV and humanity's destroyed itself?"

I was whining, but I couldn't help myself. My world was about to end. Or more like freeze.

"That's silly, Jennifer. Who'd be there to wake you?" My mom shot me an annoyed look. Sleeping on the hospital couch had made her usually perfect hair frizzy. She looked worse than me, and I could barely move.

I crossed my arms. "Aliens."

Timmy spewed orange juice from his nose and laughed. He was too young to understand what was really going on. He kept calling me Sleeping Beauty, like some prince would kiss me and wake me. Yeah, that would happen right after he became a Transformer and flew to outer space.

Mom shook her head and pulled some napkins out of a dispenser in the wall. She bent down and wiped Timmy's orange juice sneeze from the floor. I would have helped her, but my leg hung in an elevated sling in a cast that looked like a giant marshmallow.

"Honey, this is no joke."

I always used comedy to deal with the hard issues. That's why my dad called me the next late-night TV host. "I don't like not knowing. Why can't I spend my final days here with you, Dad, and Timmy?"

"Jenny, think about your dreams for the future. Where is the girl who wanted to go on safari, to work for National Geographic saving

African elephants and polar bears? Why can't you wait a few years and have a lifetime instead?"

"Because the whole thing's a big question mark. Who knows when they'll find a cure? What if *you* had to go to sleep not knowing what year you'd wake up?"

The idea scared me more than death itself. If I could have moved, I'd have bolted straight out of my hospital room and hidden in the trunk of my pink Lexus. I couldn't imagine what it would feel like to be frozen, my body suspended indefinitely until they found a cure.

"I'd sit tight and wait it out." Mom fluffed the Peruvian lilies from Aunt Lucy and dusted off the windowsill. She used cleaning to deal with issues. "The scientists are breaking new ground every day. Your father's been funding a major research team ever since you got sick."

Dad had always bought me everything I wanted. I was the only girl in my class to have a real pony, a hundred-gallon salt water aquarium on my thirteenth birthday, and a Lexus at sweet sixteen. But try as he might, he couldn't buy me more life, just a frozen forever.

Speaking of the richest man in New England, my dad walked in with Dr. Resin. He still wore his business suit from work, and Dr. Resin looked more like a gimmicky TV show ad than a true doctor. He had plasticky Ken-doll hair and a tan, which was hard to get in midwinter Maine.

"Hi, honey." My dad squeezed my hand before ruffling Timmy's hair and giving my mom a kiss on the cheek. "I've been speaking with Dr. Resin here, and he says they can start the process right away."

My mom stood up and clapped her hands together like he'd cured me. "That's wonderful news. I don't want it to spread any further."

Dr. Resin stood in the back with his hands crossed. "The longer you wait, the harder it will be. She weakens every day, and she must be as healthy and strong as possible to undergo the procedure."

My mom hugged Timmy against her. "Dr. Resin, one thing we glossed over in our last discussion was the results. How many people have successfully undergone this treatment process?"

The doctor blinked and hesitated. "This procedure is still in the experimental stages. A few test subjects have begun the process, but the completion of the treatment depends on when cures are found for their personal illnesses."

I started to jerk up in bed, but only my head moved. That small motion sent a sharp pain down my neck. "No one's ever woken up?"

"Now, honey, we have every reason to believe this works."

"Dad, I'd rather have my few more weeks in bed than freeze forever!"

Timmy gasped and pulled on my mom's arm. "Jenny's gonna freeze foreva?"

"Jennifer!" My mom's voice was harsh. "You're scaring Timmy."

"You're scaring *me*! What if I'm stuck in the middle of a nightmare the whole time? What if they can't wake me up?"

Dr. Resin pushed by my dad to stand in the middle of the room. "Let's all calm down." He turned to me and picked up my chart off the foot of the bed. "First of all, you don't freeze. The cryoprotectants administered into your body harden like glass to prevent any damaging ice crystals. All brain activity ceases in cryosleep. You won't dream. It's a painless, pleasant procedure. If I were you, I'd give it a try."

He made it sound like he was offering a new ice cream flavor. *Next time, try caramel.* The truth was, I'd be in the freezer *with* the ice cream. "I hate being cold."

After scanning my chart, his blue eyes pierced me like ice. "This is not a decision between one procedure or another. In your case, this is your only chance."

CHAPTER TWO

Fractured World

It all started because I forgot my sneakers for gym. Angela handed me an extra pair of hers from her collection. She loved track as much as I loved *National Geographic* specials and she had sneakers for running on pavement, running in the rain, and running uphill. I'm surprised she didn't have a pair for running while being sick of gym. Then again, Angela was never sick of gym.

"They look like small boats."

"I'm a whole size bigger and four inches taller." She wiggled her nose. "Put on an extra pair of socks, and you'll be fine."

"I'll fall on my butt right in front of Chad Foster."

"Maybe then he'll notice you exist."

I stared, shooting lasers at her head of teased dark curls.

She shrugged it off, reaching for her sweatshirt with her elegantly long arms. "It's better than getting a failing grade for the day."

I wished I'd put her expensive sneakers back on the shelf. In the moment, a failing grade would have been the end of my world. But looking back on it, I would have enjoyed a few more weeks of innocence much more. In cryosleep, no one considered my junior-year gym grade.

As we walked out onto the gym floor, the volleyball net came into view and my heart sank. I hated volleyball. I was always afraid I'd break a finger or bruise my arm when I served. That's why I ran *away* from the ball.

Our gym teacher, Mr. Gold, had muscles that could have been made out of gold. He was an Olympian back in the 90s. Ridgewood Prep had only the best of the best, which usually worked in my favor, except for gym. Mr. Gold didn't understand why you couldn't do three hundred pull-ups or run a mile in under six minutes. It took me a whopping ten.

So the game began. Chad served to our team, and Angela sprinted to the right, hitting the ball up over my head and back to the other side of the net. My reprieve was short-lived. Chad's best bud, Walter, hit the volleyball back, way over Angela's head and right to me. My eyes went to Angela, but she had a look that said, "Not this time. You're on your own."

So I did what I usually did. I ran away. Taking a leap backward, I tripped over the toe of my right sneaker and fell on top of my left leg in an embarrassing tumble. The ball hit the floor beside me.

Pain shot up my leg into my lower back. The bone in my lower leg felt like a toothpick split in two. I bit down, trying not to cry in front of everyone.

Angela ran to my side. "Are you okay?"

"No." I whispered under my breath, "I don't think I can get up."

"What?"

Mr. Gold shouted from across the gym. "What's going on over there?"

Angela spoke for me. "Jennifer can't stand up."

I loved my friend more than ever in that moment. Even though I'd just lost a point for our team because of my cowardice, she still defended me.

Mr. Gold walked over, disbelief clouding his eyes.

I wished I hadn't cried wolf all those other days, getting out of gym for having a phantom headache or vague dizziness that only came during third period.

"Can't get up?" He crossed his muscled arms. Tripping over yourself and falling so hard you couldn't get back up at the ripe age of seventeen was ridiculous. I knew that. Only, this time I wasn't faking.

The other students surrounded us. Spying Chad's red football jersey out of the corner of my eye made heat travel up the back of my neck to my cheeks. I couldn't lie on the gym floor forever.

I whispered to Angela, "Help me."

She pulled on my arm, but when I placed weight on my left leg, the pain exploded in an unbearable spike. I screamed like those girls in the cheap, B-horror movies.

That must have sounded believable because Mr. Gold winced and nodded to Angela. "Get the nurse."

"Yes, Coach." She patted my arm. "I'll be right back."

Meanwhile, everyone stood around me in an awkward circle.

Chad shifted on his feet. "Can we finish the game now?"

Humiliation tingled up my spine. I hated him for being so inconsiderate, but I hated myself more for liking him in the first place. Sometimes beautiful-looking people became ugly when you got to know them inside, and Chad had just turned from hottie into jerkwad. Hot tears stung my eyes.

Mr. Gold had enough sense to call off the game. "Come on, guys. The show's over. We'll continue this game tomorrow. Do your laps for the rest of class."

As the class moaned and started to run, Angela came back with Nurse Sherry. She knelt down beside me. Smiley faces dotted her scrubs, mocking me with their happiness.

"Can I take a look?"

"Sure. Go ahead. I'm not going anywhere."

Angela laughed, then covered her mouth like "I shouldn't be joking in a time like this." This was the exact sort of time I needed humor the most.

Miss Sherry probed my leg gently with her wrinkled hands. Every part she touched hurt, some more than others. I kept squirming and yelping like a baby.

She stood and stared at Mr. Gold like his gym policies had pushed me over the edge. "It's broken, all right. I'll call an ambulance."

Broken? Like, actually broken? Suddenly I didn't feel so bad about being such a crybaby.

Angela put her arm around me. "Now I see why you're so afraid of gym. You knew, Jenny. You have ESP."

I laughed despite the pain. "More like a lack of ESPN."

Angela stayed with me until the ambulance came. Nurse Sherry wrote her a note to get out of fourth period. I guess she pitied me.

The sirens wailed from the back exit doors of the gym.

Angela smiled, but she looked sad. "Our limo awaits."

"You're coming, too?"

"I've always wanted to see BMC."

I rolled my eyes as EMTs picked me up and put me on a stretcher. "I think I'll just about die if anyone sees me carried out like this."

Angela had a sparkle in her eye. "Think of it this way—it adds to your mysterious persona. You'll be the talk of the school."

"I fall down and you turn into quite the comedian."

She laughed and winked. "I have a good teacher."

CHAPTER THREE

Haunted

The doctor walked in holding X-rays underneath his arm. Unlike Dr. Resin, this man looked like a doctor, with wispy gray hair, round spectacles, and rings underneath his eyes. He was the real deal.

My mom had come from a meeting, and she sat in her pencil skirt and ruffled blouse with Angela in the metal chairs beside my bed.

"I've been reviewing your files and your X-rays, and I've got some difficult news."

Just the look on the doctor's face made my stomach twist. Right then I knew. I'd eluded it for years, but it always hung in the corner of my consciousness as a dark inevitability.

He clipped up the X-ray and clicked on the switch. An ugly black clot lay right where my leg had split. "The cancer's come back."

Emptiness barreled a hole through my heart. My mom gasped and clutched her chest with her palm, wrinkling her nicely pressed floral shirt. She reached out with her other arm and squeezed my hand, but her fingers felt brittle around mine. "Oh, honey."

The doctor continued before the barrage of questions came. "We went ahead and had multiple X-rays and a PET scan."

He clipped up a few more, but I couldn't stand to look at them. I stared at my broken leg instead.

"It's spread up her leg to her spine and from there to several of her organs, including her liver and kidneys." He stood there and waited for us to digest the bad news.

"What do you mean, it's back?" Angela stared at me like I'd lied to her all this time. I had. I wanted to be considered normal. I didn't want pity friends.

"I'm sorry."

"You never told me."

I shrugged, regretting bringing her into the hospital room. I didn't want her to have to suffer like me. "I thought you might have seen the episode of *American Idol.*"

Angela's eyes widened. "You were a contestant on *American Idol,* and you didn't tell me that either?"

"No, no, no." I shook my head. If it was any other afternoon, I would have laughed out loud instead of verging on tears. "I had osteosarcoma as a kid, a nasty bone cancer. They cured me. I was cancer-free for seven years. *American Idol* did a special where the contestants serenaded sick kids. There was a segment about me and my family."

She shook her head, tears running down her face. "I never saw it. Geez, isn't that something you'd tell your best friend?"

My mom interrupted us to ask the doctor what I was too afraid to ask myself. "Can she beat the cancer again?"

He shook his head and shut off the X-ray screen. "The cancer has progressed to stage four, ma'am. It's not likely."

I glanced at my body. My limbs looked so fragile and thin underneath the hospital gown. I'd been queasy the last few weeks. I forced myself to sit up straighter as if I could will him to be wrong. "I feel fine."

His mouth was a thin line. "Many people do until the last few weeks."

I thought about Timmy, my mom, Angela, and my dad. I wanted to be there for them. I didn't want to leave them behind.

"Is there anything we can do?" My mind scrambled around all the different treatments I'd heard of. "Chemotherapy, lasers, drugs, anything?"

His face was as blank as a mask. I wondered if he felt anything underneath his clinical façade.

I hated him for being so businesslike.

"I'm sorry, but it's too late."

The anger swirled up inside me like a tornado waiting to strike. I wanted to throw my pillow at him, or maybe something a little harder, like a shoe. I'd already dealt with this and now I had to do it again. Except this time there was no winning.

My mom must have seen the anguish in my face. The earlier bout had almost killed me, reducing me to a skeleton. I'd used all of my courage to fight it, and I wasn't sure I had anything left to give.

She wrapped her arm around me and we faced the doctor together. "I'm not going to take no for an answer. We've beat it before, and we'll do it again. Money is not an issue."

The doctor rubbed his eyes and his chin, like he'd gone through this a thousand times before with a thousand other unlucky girls like me. "Well, there's an experimental technology being developed right now. It's highly controversial and very expensive. Truthfully, I'm not sure anything will come of it."

My mom nodded at me like she'd fix it just like she fixed my Lexus when I crashed it into the neighbor's mailbox. It had a shiny new fender the next day.

"Sign her up."

CHAPTER FOUR

Preparations

Mom, Dad, and Timmy visited my bedside before the doctors put me to sleep. Although none of us knew how long I'd be frozen, their red-rimmed eyes and long faces looked like they were saying good-bye for forever.

Timmy ran up to my bed and hugged my head with his little arms. "Bye, Jenny. I'm going to miss you."

"Bye, Timmy. I'll miss you, too, little guy." Tears stung my eyes, but I held them back because I didn't want to upset him. "Make sure you brush your teeth like Mom says, and no more putting your action figures in the radiator, okay?"

He sniffed and wiped his eyes. "I guess so."

With his head of curly blond hair and ruby-red cheeks, he looked like one of those tots on the Welch's grape juice commercials. I wanted to remember him like this—perfect, even though he bent my hairclips and wiped mouthfuls of peanut butter on my bath towel.

Mom hugged me next.

"Remember to feed my fish, and make sure Thunderbolt gets groomed regularly. Grit gets stuck underneath his shoes."

"Of course, dear." She pulled away and shrugged. "Who knows, they might wake you up next year."

She laughed, but I think we both knew it would be longer than that.

"Hopefully I won't miss too much." Big events passed by in flashes of thought—the next Disney cruise, Mom's run for mayor in two years, Timmy's first day of school, Dad's retirement party. I didn't want to miss any of it. I couldn't think about timelines anymore, or I'd make myself sick.

Dad squeezed my hand and kissed my cheek. "I've spoken with the world's top doctors, and they are on the verge of a cure. I know this will work, honey. You have to believe me."

"Yes, Dad." I believed him. Modern science didn't disappoint, especially when funded by significant dollar signs. It was just that I didn't know when. What if my friends were all grown up and my hair was out of style? I imagined Angela as a middle-aged woman shopping with a teenage me in the mall, and it didn't seem right. She'd probably have a life of her own, kids of her own. Why would she want to hang out with me anymore?

Or maybe I'd wake up and Timmy would be my age. We could be best buds and finish school together, double date for the prom. That'd be awesome. No more fights about letting him watch SpongeBob.

Dr. Resin came in. "The chamber is ready. It's time."

My pulse quickened. My life was one of those hourglasses, and the last few grains had run out. I'd already said goodbye to Angela because the policy said family only in the cryo lab, but now I thought of a thousand more things I wanted to tell her. "Can I talk to Angela one more time?"

Dr. Resin's mouth set in a firm line. "We must proceed immediately while the cryo chamber settings are optimal."

I scanned all the eyes around me. "I'm not ready yet."

Resin wheeled my bed to the door. "It's best not to dwell on good-byes."

I reached out to grab Timmy's hand. Mom held him back, crying silent tears, while Dad saluted me with his stoic face and dark eyes. "Remember we love you, and when you wake up, you'll be cured. You'll be free."

My heart beat a thousand times a minute as Resin pushed me down the corridor to a new wing labeled *Cryonics Institute of New England*. I wanted to yell for someone to help me, but I knew none of the nurses would answer my pleas. They scurried by, like I was an afterthought in their world. And I was.

The cryosleep chamber looked like a giant spaceship from *Star Trek*. Tubes ran around the vacuum chamber, surrounding the hull like dreadlocks, all thick and twisted. A monitor beeped on top with a temperature gauge that read eighteen degrees Celsius. It was hard to imagine the inside would drop to negative one hundred and twenty-eight. Beneath the monitor, a small window the size of a cereal box revealed wires spewing everywhere and a faint blue light. At least I didn't have to sleep in the dark.

A hatch lifted. I expected misty air to pour out, but nothing happened. The nurses surrounded me and rubbed alcohol on my arms and legs.

I tried not to think about the liquid nitrogen that would flood the capsule, stopping any physical decay. I imagined floating inside it and remembered reading how bodies sink to the bottom because of their density. My throat felt fuzzy, and I thought I'd throw up. I hadn't been allowed to eat anything the last twenty-four hours, so there was nothing left anyway.

A nurse attached tubes to my arms and legs with needles that pricked my skin. I stared at her questioningly, and she patted my head. "These are for the cryo-protectants, my dear."

My voice squeaked out, "Will it hurt?"

"No, no." Another nurse pricked my arm with another needle. "You'll be asleep before we start the process."

I released my breath, wondering how many more I had.

"Count down from ten, dear."

I looked at her like she was crazy. Count down from ten? That was not how I wanted to spend my last few moments awake.

The anesthesiologist put a mask over my face.

10 Mom looked so sad.
9 Will Timmy remember me?
8 Angela, where the hell are you?
7 My feet are getting cold.
6 The lights are so bright.

I didn't even get to five.

CHAPTER FIVE

Awake

Suspended animation in cryosleep was like the time before I was born. Darkness and nothing. I don't even remember being cold.

I woke up to a hazy silhouette lurking around my bed. My eyes couldn't adjust to the light, no matter how much I rubbed them. My body felt light, and my leg moved freely. The cast had been stripped off. Most of all, I felt no pain for the first time since the accident in gym class. No pain. In fact, I felt great, like I could run a mile and beat Mr. Gold's high standards. Had I died and gone to heaven?

"Don't worry, sweetie. Your eyesight will return in time." It was the voice of an older woman. She patted down my hair. "You've had quite the sleep."

It felt like only minutes had passed since I fell asleep. Maybe I wasn't out for that long. "Can I see my family?"

"Right now, you must rest." Her voice grew stern.

I blinked.

"Dr. Kline will be in later to discuss the specifics."

"Dr. Kline?" I thrashed my arms around to find her, but the sound of footsteps grew faint. "Where's Dr. Resin?" For once, I was eager to see him.

"Your new doctor is Dr. Kline."

The door clicked closed, and then a monitor pulsed by my bed. My legs were cold, so I reached for a sheet, but there was nothing there. I lay on a cushioned surface.

Even the pillow was built into the frame. How was I supposed to sleep without my arm under my pillow? I couldn't go anywhere half-blind, so I closed my eyes, waiting for this mysterious Dr. Kline. I'd had so many doctors over the years, their names and faces blended together like a police lineup, with Dr. Resin right at the top. *But he was right. I'm awake, alive.*

Anxiety and anticipation spread throughout my body in eager little bubbles, like my veins were filled with Mountain Dew. I tapped my fingers to the same rhythm over and over to keep busy. I couldn't wait to get home and ride Thunderbolt, tease Timmy, and eat a giant bowl of chocolate ice cream.

The door opened and I squinted to focus. The vague shadows gave way to faint blurriness. I made out the face of a middle-aged man with dark hair.

"How's my new patient doing?"

I sat up on the bed and bent forward to read his expression. "Dr. Kline?"

"That's right." He took a seat beside my bed and brought out a device that looked like an iPhone. "Your results look good, my girl. As you've probably already noticed, after we reanimated your body, we healed your leg and cured the cancer. You're one hundred percent cancer-free."

The burden clenching my chest lifted and I bit my tongue to keep from crying. "A lot has happened while I've been asleep, hasn't it?"

His eyes flickered as if he held something back. "You could say that, yes."

"How long have I been frozen?"

Dr. Kline rose and put the iPhone beside the bed. "Let's invite your family in. I think it's best they fill you in on specifics."

He stuck his head out the door and gestured to someone down the hall. I wiggled both feet while waiting, marveling at how I was still alive. Life seemed too good to be true, and I soaked it in, savoring each moment I breathed without pain.

A man walked in beside the doctor. He was the same age as my dad and had the same dark eyes, prominent nose and rugged chin, but curly blond hair covered his head. Could my dad have changed his hairstyle? It didn't seem very businesslike.

I stuttered, "Dad?" *No wait. What if Timmy was all grown up?* "Timmy?" I wished I could see clearly.

The man walked around the bed and sat beside me. He was neither of them and both of them at the same time.

"David and Timothy Streetwater are my ancestors."

The room rushed around me like a washing machine on high cycle. My mind wrestled with his words, wrapping itself around them and denying it. "Where's Timmy? Where are my mom and dad?"

"Dr. Kline said it would be hard on you." He took my hand and squeezed it. "I want you to know, I'm so glad you're alive. My wife and I have adopted you. We're your legal guardians now. My name is Valex Streetwater, and my wife is Len."

Valex? Len? Did everyone's name sound like a household cleaner? What happened to all the Marys and Toms? "What year is it?" I demanded, bracing myself.

Valex glanced at Doctor Kline and the doctor shook his head in a subtle *no*. Valex patted my arm. "We'll get to that." He gestured to a woman out in the hall, "Why don't you come in now, honey?"

An Asian woman with long, shiny black hair peeked in. She wore a bright pink dress that looked so straight it must have been made out of paper. That's when I realized Valex's clothes were strange as well. He wore a gold tunic with a yellow dot in the middle. My eyes were getting better by the minute, but I didn't like what I saw.

The Asian woman stepped in. "Are you sure?"

Valex turned to me and lifted an eyebrow. "Do you want to meet her?"

My stomach flipped. That giant bowl of chocolate ice cream didn't seem so appetizing any more. I'd woken up on the wrong side of the bed, or fallen into an alternate universe, like on *The Twilight Zone*. I squeezed my eyes shut and wished it all away. *Please, please, please be a dream.*

When I opened my eyes, Valex still sat beside me, waiting for my response. When I looked into his eyes, I saw my dad, and when I studied each curl, I saw Timmy. My mom's thin, arched brows were his as well, along with Grandpa's cheekbones. I reached out and touched a stray end of his hair. "You look just like them." My voice shook.

"I'll be there for you, just like they were."

Anger rose inside me and struck out like a lightning bolt. "No. I want to go home."

Dr. Kline pushed between us as if he could take back my harsh voice. "She's had enough for today." He yanked on Valex's arm until he stood. "We have counsellors available to help her. Let's let her digest this new information."

"We're just going to leave her here?"

Dr. Kline ushered Valex out of the room.

Part of me wanted him to stay because he reminded me so much of Timmy and Dad, and another part of me couldn't bear to look at him. He was proof my world was gone.

"She's due to stay and speak to counsellors while we monitor her condition." He whispered under his breath, but his voice carried. "We have a high suicide rate with woken cryosleepers. You may pick her up when she's come to terms with her status."

Valex spoke over his shoulder. "Get some rest. We'll be back for you when you're ready."

I had no words. My entire body was in denial, shock jarring me until nothing made sense.

After the door shut behind them, I couldn't hold back the tears. They came like a tidal wave, soaking the front of my hospital gown. I pounded my fists on the bed, thinking of all the things I'd missed. Now that I was alive and healthy, I didn't want to go on. What was the point?

A nurse scuttled in and pressed a needle into my arm. The hospital room disappeared around me into the endless oblivion from which I came.

CHAPTER SIX

Alone

I clutched Thunderbolt's reins with sweaty palms as he pounded the earth. The sun set in a bright fire bath on the horizon, and I raced to meet it, as if catching the brilliant gold could somehow take back time.

The scent of his mane mingled with the freshly cut grass of our pasture. I drew in a long breath, filling my lungs. We rode so hard that I lost myself in the rhythm of his hoofbeats, as if our bodies melded into one and nothing else existed. Freedom and exhilaration washed over me like spring rain.

"Come on, Thunderbolt, faster!" I nudged my heels in his flanks.

Thunderbolt whinnied and bolted ahead. The rhythm stuttered like a weakening heartbeat. Had he missed a step?

I tumbled forward into a heap of arms and legs. I braced myself to be buried underneath his weight, or trampled by his hooves. The air whooshed over my head as he leapt over me, racing toward the setting sun.

"Thunderbolt, wait for me."

When I scrambled to stand, pain shot down my leg. Somehow, a cast had formed around it, weighing me down. A nurse stood beside me, as if she worked in the meadow every day.

"We've got to get you to the recovery room." She bent down and lifted me onto a rolling bed. All I cared about was Thunderbolt getting away.

I pointed. "Over there. We have to go after him. There's no fence and he could run away."

"Yes, my dear." She pushed the bed forward.

The grass made it bumpy and slow. "Hurry up."

"There's no rush, dear. You'll be woken in due time."

Woken? Was I asleep? Was this a dream?

When we got to the edge of the meadow, the sun had set. Twilight hung over me in a cold haze. I shivered, clutching my shoulders. I scanned the horizon and saw a black rump sticking out of a cluster of trees. "Over there."

As she pushed me forward, her face turned into Mom's perfect fox-like features. A swirl of emotion threatened to crumple me, and I couldn't figure out why I needed her so badly. Wouldn't I see her at dinner?

"Mom, we have to get Thunderbolt."

"Yes, Jennifer. We're almost there."

His black hide glistened in the moonlight. She was right.

"Thunderbolt, over here." I clicked my tongue. He always came when I made that noise, because I had treats.

I shoved my hands in my pockets, but they were empty. When had I used all the treats?

I whistled, and Thunderbolt didn't move.

Mom seemed oblivious. "Who knows, they might wake you up in a year."

"What?" I reached out and touched Thunderbolt's hide. The fur was cold and coarse. My heart raced, and I swallowed a rising current of dread. I leaned over so far I almost fell off the bed and stretched my arms. My fingers caught around the saddle. I yanked him out of the trees and screamed.

A stuffed horse fell on the grass below my bed. His glass eyes stared at me as if asking why I abandoned him. I rubbed the hand that had touched his hide on my good leg to wipe away the feeling of his fake skin, but the feeling of the dead hair kept coming back and my spine tingled.

"Mom, how could you let me sleep for so long?"

When I turned around, she was gone.

I awoke shivering and reached for my sheets. My hands groped in the dark and closed on air. Had I kicked them off? Why was my pillow stuck down?

My eyes adjusted to the green light of the heart monitor, and my horrible day rushed back like a slap in the face. I relived the horrors of learning everyone I knew was dead. It left me with an emptiness so large it could eat me alive. I wanted to squirm it off, but it clung to me like mold.

I cried until I had no tears left and my stomach muscles hurt from sobbing. I felt so alone that I could have been the last person alive on Earth. Curling up into a fetal position, I wanted to feel Mom's arms around me, hear the sound of Dad's voice. All those times Timmy wanted me to play cars with him on the floor and I said no hurt like stabs in my heart. I was too interested in my stuff, the latest gossip in school, and shopping. How could I have been so distracted?

In the middle of the night in my futuristic hospital room, I finally realized what was important in life. Not some school dance, my gym grade, or the latest accessory from Abercrombie. When everything was stripped away, family and the people you cared about were all that mattered. Too bad I realized it too late.

"Wake me up." I cried out loud to whoever would listen. "Get me out of here."

No one answered. Only the beeping of the heart monitor, and it always said the same thing. The emptiness was so complete that I could have died right there and not cared. But that's not what my family would have wanted. They invested all of their money and hopes on this project, and it worked.

To fight the depression, I had to keep going. I owed it to them.

They'd want me to give this new world a chance. If anything, I couldn't let the thousands of dollars Dad had paid for me to have this second chance go to waste. Besides, I couldn't lie in BMC forever. I hated hospitals. Anything would be better than this, even if I had to put up with people I didn't know, people who looked like they'd stolen my family's faces right off them.

I reached around the bed for the button to hail the nurse, but the sleek chrome had no panels.

"Damn. Stupid futuristic bed."

How did they call people on *Star Trek*? I cleared my throat. "Computer, get me the nurse." I felt like the biggest geek ever, but after a second, the wall on my left flicked on like a giant TV. I jerked back, expecting something to explode. An older woman's face peered at me.

"Yes?"

Um. Do I just talk to the wall?

The older woman tilted her head. "You hailed?"

My voice came out as a mouse shriek. "Yes."

"Is anything wrong?"

"No."

It took me a moment to remember the weird names of my new legal guardians. "Call Valex and Len Streetwater. I don't need to talk to the counselors. I'm ready to go home."

CHAPTER SEVEN

Metropolis

I dragged my feet like a zombie, following Valex and Len through the corridors of the Cryonics Institute of New England. Dr. Resin's picture hung on the wall along with a plaque that said, *Founding Father 1967-2064*. He smiled like a movie star thanking his adoring public. He'd slicked his hair back in a luscious wave of blond, and his tan was the color of my mom's coffee. Easy for him. He wasn't the one that had to go on in a world where everything had changed. It would have been much easier to die that day with my family by my bedside. But I owed it to them to keep going.

I wasn't alone. Valex picked up my bags, along with a few storage containers of items my family had left for me. Len held my hand and gently nudged me along with kind words. Her tiny hand had so much strength in it that I couldn't refuse her.

Valex caught me mentally smiting Dr. Resin and smiled. "Let's go, Jennifer. Our ride is just beyond that gate."

"Don't we have to take the stairs down?" If I remembered correctly, the New England Cryogenics Institute was on the tenth floor of BMC.

Valex shook his head and winked his dark eye. "We don't need any stairs."

Len poked him in the side with her finger. "Don't tease her. She's had a hard day."

"What?" I huffed. "What am I missing?"

Valex tilted his head toward the door. "Come on. It's much easier to show you than explain."

Valex was way more easygoing than my dad. Comparing the two of them sent a shot of pain directly to my heart, and I closed down my memories in order to survive and keep walking. No matter how cool Valex was, he could never replace my real dad.

Valex pressed a panel and the door slid open. We walked out onto a dock where strange ships with no wheels stood in rows and the sky opened up above us. Valex dug in his pocket and pulled out a black box. He pressed a button and a *beep* sounded from the third ship down the line, a small aerodynamic-looking bubble with striped wings.

"You own a spaceship!"

Valex nodded. "Yup. But it's not a spaceship. It's a hovercraft."

"Wow."

Len rolled her eyes and took my arm. "Everyone has one. Come on. He's just being a show-off."

The hatch lifted and we crowded in. Valex put my bags in the back and took up the controls. When the ship turned on, seat restraints came down, belting us in automatically. I jerked away and Valex and Len laughed. "The seat belts won't hurt you."

Great. Just my comeuppance. Now I was stuck with two parent comedians to tease me. I wanted to tell them how I used to be smart and witty, but the words stuck on my tongue and I sat in silence as the hovercraft took off.

Bath, Maine, looked more like New York City on a Monday morning. Instead of rural barn houses and fields, high-rise buildings crowded the skyline. There was no ground anywhere, and I realized why everyone flew in hovercrafts. The buildings were so close together that there were no roads.

"Where are all the fields?"

"They grow the crops on top of the high-rises." Len pointed to bubble-shaped greenhouses capping each skyscraper like the tops of vegan slushies.

"You mean there's no ground?"

Valex laughed. He turned a fast corner and the ship sped forward. "Of course there's ground. What do you think the buildings are built on?"

I took a deep breath and re-phrased the question. "I mean no grass, no fields?"

Len turned around and stared at me like that was the oddest question she'd ever heard. I thought it was pretty normal, considering.

"Well?"

Valex leaned over to Len. "Back in Jennifer's time, the population was only a smidgen of what it is now. We have to remember that."

Len nodded and fidgeted with her fuchsia wristbands.

I looked at her expectantly, but she turned back to Valex.

His hands tightened on the controls. "I'm sorry. By the time the doctors found us, you were already undergoing treatment. We didn't have very long to plan. We haven't done any research from your time. All I know is from an early twenty-first-century course I took in college. I haven't even given much thought as to how to tell you about…the advancements."

"Advancements?" It seemed like humanity had gone backward, or spiraled down a hole they couldn't get out of.

Valex blinked, and his jaw hardened as if he'd made up his mind. "The world's a lot different now. It's not all bad. We've cured so many diseases, people live much longer than they used to, and our population is thriving. We've had to make changes to support our growing needs."

"What year is it, exactly?" They'd veered around the question in the hospital, but with Doctor Kline out of the picture, I hoped they'd come clean.

"Twenty-three-fourteen." Valex said it like he'd said the time was 2:30.

The year was so different than what I was used to, it took me a whole minute to calculate.

"You're kidding me. Three hundred and two years?"

My family was gone—that I knew—because Valex and Len wouldn't have picked me up. But, I couldn't think about them now. Instead, I thought of everyone else from my century, including Taylor Swift, Johnny Depp, President Obama, even the voice of SpongeBob.

They were long dead, like not even bones in the ground. Valex and Len probably didn't even know who SpongeBob was, although I bet they'd learned about Obama in the history books.

Len reached behind her and put a hand on my arm, "Let's not discuss this now. You've already had such a hard day. Try to enjoy the trip."

I nodded and she pointed over the dashboard. "Over there you have the Delta Ray Towers. They were built twenty years ago, when I was a child, to house hundreds more people here in Bath. Over here are the communications headquarters. They supply the needs of the entire city. The power plant is over there, and that building is a recycling center."

Her voice soothed me. I sat back and listened, pretending I was on a tour for one of our Disney vacations, like if the Jetsons had a theme park ride. I know I was living in denial, but it was the only way I could keep going without a total shutdown.

After twenty minutes, they landed on a loading dock and Len announced, "We're home."

I grabbed one of my bags and Valex took it right out of my hands. "No, no, no. You're the guest today. Let me."

I shrugged and let them carry everything. Len led me to their part of floor two hundred and thirty-seven.

Geez. How tall would the buildings get? I reminded myself not to look down whenever I looked out the window.

Valex inserted a key card into the door. "I already have a spare one for you."

Like I was going anywhere? It took me three tries to pass my driver's ed test, never mind knowing how to fly one of those hovercrafts.

Len shouted over my shoulder. "Pell, we're home!"

A little girl skittered around the corner and stared open-mouthed. She had pigtails of wispy black hair and dark, almond-shaped eyes. She wore a silver tunic that looked like it was made out of tin foil, with fuzzy pink slippers.

"You brought me home just what I wanted." She ran over to me and hugged my legs before I could get away. The feeling of her little hands on me reminded me so much of Timmy that I had to lean onto the wall to keep from passing out with grief. "My very own big sister!"

"Hey now, give Jennifer some space. She's had a long day."

Guilt rolled over me for not reacting with the same excitement she had.

"We apologize for Pell's forwardness." Len winked. "She gets it from Valex."

Valex tickled Len's arm and laughed. "I'm sure she'll calm down once she gets to know you."

I tried to move, but she clung so hard I was afraid I might kick her, so I just stood there like an awkward teenager at a lame dance.

Len gave me a sympathetic smile. "Pell, you have to let go."

"I don't want to. I'm afraid she'll run away and I'll be stuck with C-7 again."

I looked around, but all I saw were strange appliances that beeped, a white couch with no cushions, and a computer monitor the size of the wall. "What is C-7?"

"He's an awful babysitter. He won't even play Pixie Swap on the wallscreen. He says it's not in his programming."

"Pell, you know he's not programmed to be unpractical." It was the first time I'd heard Len's voice turn stern. I wondered if this was an ongoing fight between the two of them.

"He's a bothead and I hate him."

Just as she said it, a silver leg appeared from behind the couch. The metal was round and smooth like the side of a pot. Another hand rubbed a cloth over a spot on the floor. The fingers were all perfect capsules that clicked on the linoleum.

"Stain removal complete." The voice sounded like the man on our GPS. As C-7 stood up, my breath caught in my throat. My eyes must have bugged out of my head, because Pell started to giggle.

Len gestured toward him. "Jennifer, meet C-7, our personal family manager."

The robot stepped over to me in a swift, gliding motion. His face was a mask of plastic with gold chrome eyes boring right into my head.

Could he see my fear?

He spoke again, and his lips moved like chopsticks clanking together. "Nice to meet you, Jennifer."

No wonder Pell hated being babysat by C-7. That thing would spook the hell outta me if I were left alone with it.

"Well, tell him hello." Pell took my hand and placed it in his cold, robotic fingers.

"Hello, C-7." I took back my hand and kneeled down so my eyes were level with Pell's. I needed to show her some attention considering how much energy she'd spent on welcoming me. It was the first step to accepting my new family. Even though they'd never replace what I had, I owed it to them to try. "Come on, if he won't play Pixie Swap with you, then I will."

She jumped up and down. "Awesomelicious with sappy sauce on top!"

I smiled for the first time all day. "Sappy-what?"

She gave me a look that said, "You're being silly," so I let it go.

"Never mind, show me how to play."

CHAPTER EIGHT

Video Logs

Pixie Swap made my brain hurt. Cute little fairies danced on the screen, teasing me. Each one balanced on a leaf, and you had to solve a math problem to get them to the other side of the pond. These weren't two plus two equations, either. Little Pell was doing long division, complicated multiplication, and even some algebra.

"How old are you?"

Pell clicked the remote with her fingers and squealed when she got it right. "I'm seven."

I looked behind me at Len, who dropped cubes into a gurgling food processor to make dinner. "She's only seven?"

"We start them on math early, nowadays. You really need to excel to get a job in the upper levels of the high-rises. Granted, Pell is ahead of the game for her age."

She smiled at her daughter, "Keep trying, Pell. You might make it to level nine tonight."

I couldn't imagine what level nine would be. Geometry? Physics?

She handed me the controls. "Your turn."

I sighed. "Let's put me on level one."

Behind me, Valex unpacked some of the containers we brought home from BMC. "Looks like you have a bunch of DVDs here, Jennifer. The discs are old, but I think I can hook up some software to decode them."

A pang hit me straight in the heart. I didn't want to think about home. "I'll watch them later."

"Certainly. I'll hook them up to the wallscreen in your room."

"Great. Thank you." I calculated forty-five plus thirty-two divided by three. My pixie flew across the pond, spreading glitter dust.

Pell clapped. "Very good!"

Although the math stretched my brain thin, I was thankful for the distraction. I'd compartmentalized my life before I woke up and locked my memories in a box in my mind. I'd deal with it later once things sank in. If I didn't think about it, maybe Timmy, Mom and Dad could still be alive somewhere in the turn of time, thinking about me, too.

"Dinner's ready," Len announced behind us.

"Aw. She's only figured out one."

Pell looked so cute when she pouted, I almost argued in her favor, but I wanted to show Len and Valex I was thankful. I stood up, setting the example. "It's okay, Pell. We'll play again later."

"You promise?"

"Of course, I promise." I wasn't going anywhere anytime soon. I was stuck in 2314 playing Pixie Swap with a seven-year-old. None of it made sense.

We sat at an oblong table with strange glowing lights overhead. I sat next to Pell, and Valex and Len sat across from us. Len heaped two piles of greenish mush on my plate along with a few cubes of white stuff.

"The flavor tonight is garden delight." She looked so proud to tell me. I had to try it.

I picked up a spork—who knew they'd eat with sporks in the future? The mush dribbled off, and I had to dig in to get a good helping. Everyone watched while I stuck it in my mouth.

The paste tasted like vegetables and spice. It wasn't bad, but it wasn't Mom's good old meat loaf and potatoes, either.

"I like it." I forced a smile as it trickled down my throat.

"Wonderful." Valex squeezed Len's shoulder.

Len smiled.

"She saved the best night for you."

What were all the other nights going to taste like? Dread rose up in my throat, and I swallowed it down. No, I couldn't make a scene at the dinner table. Not in front of Pell. I had to be strong. I spooned up another bite.

"What's it made out of?"

Len popped a white cube in her mouth like a chip. "Soybeans. The majority of our food is manufactured from soybeans and vegetables. Soy is incredibly versatile. They've even perfected an allergy-free strain."

"You mean you're vegetarians?"

Valex laughed. "You make it sound like we've got a computer virus. Everyone is vegetarian. It's better for you, and we simply don't have enough room for livestock anymore."

"Where are all the animals?" My voice squeaked. An imaginary coil suffocated my throat, and I struggled to breathe. My worst nightmare was coming true and I couldn't wake up. I was already awake.

"They're extinct." Pell said it like a fact she learned in school. "Everyone knows that, dumb-bot."

"Pell," Valex gave her a stern look. "Jennifer isn't from our time. Where she grew up, they had tons of animals."

Thunderbolt's glassy eye staring at me stuck in my mind. I winced and shook my head, but the memory was permanent.

Pell gasped and dropped her spork. "You got to touch real animals?"

Tears brimmed. A maelstrom of emotion swirled in my stomach and the room blurred through my tears. I was doing so well hiding the pain, and now it poured out of me. I could barely speak. "I did."

"Oh, Jennifer." Len reached for me across the table. "I'm so sorry. We shouldn't have brought it up."

Everyone gawked at me. The table pushed into my stomach and my plate of food had coalesced into gel. All at once I felt sick. The lives of all the dogs, kittens, polar bears, whales, moose, doves, turtles… every animal I could think of flashed before my eyes, blinking out of existence in a silent scream.

"What happened to the animals?"

Everyone fell silent like none of them wanted to talk about it. But they'd already told me the horrible news and broken my heart. I had to know why.

"Well?"

Valex placed his spork on the table. As the head of the family, I guess it was his job to explain. "Little by little, humans took up more space, and we had to make decisions. Big animals consumed too many resources. Livestock were fed more than three times the human-edible grain than what their bodies produced in meat."

"So what did they do to all the animals? Kill them?"

"Over time it cost too much to breed them, so they died off naturally."

I dropped my spork on the table. "There's nothing natural about it."

Pell froze as if unsure who to believe.

Len glanced at me, and then at Pell. "Jenny, please. You're scaring Pell."

I stared at her in disbelief. She was calling me out for scaring Pell? Sure, Pell was too young to understand, but Valex and Len could have more sympathy. I may have expected the cold response from Len, with her "everything's perfect" attitude, but from Valex? I had to remind myself that Valex hadn't killed all of the animals; he was simply a product of his generation. Most likely, when he was born they were already all dead or goners to be sure. Still, his laid-back manner about everything hit a sour chord with this. How could he be so okay with it?

What I couldn't fathom was how humans didn't stand up for the animals. Guess we had picked our own kind over theirs.

Disgust brought up bile from my stomach. "Excuse me. I'm sorry." I stood up and my chair screeched backward.

Len moved to rise, but Valex waved her down. "Your room is the first door panel down that hall. Take all the time you need."

"Thank you."

I stumbled down the hall and dull blue lights flickered on, sensing my presence. I wanted to run away from the world, but I settled for my new room. I pushed the door panel, like I'd seen Valex do earlier, and the wall fizzled out, revealing a small bed like the one in the hospital. *Great, no sheets.* A stark white desk protruded from the wall. Valex had stacked my containers on top of it. He'd opened the DVD cases and flipped through them. They were numbered one to thirty-one. Dread settled like a cold rock in my stomach. What had happened to make them stop? I'd have to watch each one to find out.

The first one was already hooked up to a cord plugged into the wall. I pressed the panel and hit the play button with my finger. The screen blinked on, casting my room in a white glow. I sat down, rocking back and forth and hugged myself, trying to calm down. Angela's face shone in front of me, and my insides almost melted into that soybean slush I tried for dinner.

Oh, Angela, where are you now when I need you the most?

She walked in front of the maple trees planted in perfect rows leading to Ridgewood Prep. "Your parents let me bring the video camera to school. I'm supposed to document what you're missing so when you wake up, you can get all caught up."

She turned the camera on three boys kicking a hacky sack. Behind them, Chad flirted with one of the cheerleaders. Turning the camera back to her, she shook her head. "So far, you're not missing much."

I laughed out loud, surprising myself. Who knew I'd get her joke three hundred years later? What did it matter? Seeing the video made me feel normal, like my life wasn't some fairy tale I made up before I got to futuristic hell.

Angela kept the video on until she got to first period and clicked it off just as Ms. Dayton wrote a trigonometry problem on the board. Thank goodness she didn't make me sit through that. The video flicked to gym class. The volleyball nets were still up in the same place as when I broke my leg. Seeing them again sent a shiver across my shoulders.

Angela turned the camera on her face. "You're never going to believe this, but Chad wants to talk to you." She focused the camera on Chad as he jogged from the sidelines in his red jersey.

Angela's voice, like a voiceover in some movie, said, "Okay, Chad, now's the time to come clean."

Chad's perfect face fell into a serious frown. "Hey, Jenny." His voice was so somber I almost didn't recognize it. He flicked back his perfect swirl of hair and took a deep breath. "About gym class the other day. I didn't mean to make light of your broken leg." His lips twisted into a mischievous smile. "Not that you're going to care when you wake up in the future and they have all kinds of cool stuff like laser swords, spaceships, robots—"

"That's enough. Jenny's not going to be asleep that long. You watch, I bet she comes back in time for prom." Angela's voice seemed so defensive, I could tell how hurt she was that I wasn't there. My chest tightened. Poor Angela.

"Whatever." Chad shrugged and jogged back to the volleyball net. "My serve!"

Angela turned the camera back on her face. "See, he's not a complete jerkwad. Just a small one."

I watched the video for the next few hours until she forgot she'd left it on in the car, and I fell asleep watching the oaks on the side of the windshield fly by in a blur.

Trees. I miss them, too.

CHAPTER NINE

Bodyguard

"**W**ake up, sleepyhead. You're going with me to school."

I opened my eyes and Pell jumped up and down beside my bed, pigtails flying like pinwheels. *How did I even get to the bed?* Valex or Len must have come in, shut off the DVD, and carried me. Usually I hated it when someone entered my room, but the thought of them looking after me actually gave me a warm, fuzzy feeling. Then I thought of my parents and the sadness rushed back in in full force.

"What's wrong? You don't wanna go?"

Let's see—new school, new people and, judging from Pell's video game, highly advanced classes way over my head.

"Actually, no." Valex and Len had said nothing about going back to school. Why didn't they tell me? Seemed like they weren't prepared for a lot of things after I woke up—including how to deal with an emotionally challenged teenager from another century. I had to remind myself they were doing the best they could. They did take me in, after all.

"That's what Mommy said you'd say." Pell giggled. "That's why she sent me." She grabbed my hand, and her little fingers crushed mine together with surprising strength. "Come on. I'll take good care of you."

"Great." I shook my head, sitting upright with my legs dangling. *I'm gonna look real cool with a seven-year-old bodyguard.* "What's for breakfast? Soy slush?"

"No, sillybot." Pell pulled me off the bed and led me into the kitchen. Today she wore a pink tunic with striped gold and purple leggings, reminding me of an Oompa Loompa. Would I have to wear something equally as hideous? "It's soycakes with sappy sauce."

"Sounds delicious."

Len stood behind the counter flipping what looked kind of like pancakes, except they were green, making my stomach quiver. I was afraid she'd mention last night's breakdown, but she smiled instead. "Good morning, Jennifer. Are you hungry?"

"Not really."

My negative attitude didn't seem to affect the bright smile on her face. "You should try eating some breakfast. You have a big day ahead of you."

I took a seat next to Pell. "Yeah, what's this about school?"

"Ridgewood Prep starts today, and I thought it'd be good for you to throw yourself right in, make yourself busy. Besides, the longer you go without school, the harder it'll be to get back into it."

"Ridgewood Prep? It still exists?"

"Of course. It's the best school in all of New England. Your parents had good taste." Len placed a plate of green soycakes in front of me. She overturned a plastic container and white goop plopped on top of the stack. Pell rubbed her hands beside me. "Yummy sappy sauce."

I picked up my spork, hating how she talked about my parents like they were on a vacation and not piles of dust. "You've already enrolled me for this year?"

"You were already enrolled. All I had to do was update your file."

I sporked a soycake. *Great. All my bad gym grades are still there, frozen for eternity like me. So much for starting with a clean slate.*

Len gave Pell a smaller plate and she dived right in, using her fingers to spread the sappy sauce. I made a mental note not to hold her sticky hand if she offered it.

"What if I refuse to go?"

Pressing the panel for the stove, Len came and sat down by me with a serious look on her face. "You don't have to do anything you don't want to. Unlike Pell, who has to work hard to get good grades for a chance at a job in the upper levels, you have it made. Your parents set aside a trust fund, which only grew over all the years you've been in cryosleep, accumulating interest. You have close to twenty billion credits, enough for ten lifetimes. You're the richest girl in New England."

Numbness tingled through me. It made perfect sense that my parents would plan ahead and secure my future. Just thinking about them made me sick with melancholy.

"Okay, then I'll stay home."

A tight smile formed on Len's face. "Great. C-7 would love your company. You can help him clean the house."

Looking over my shoulder, I saw C-7 perk his head up. A shiver ran through my arms. I had nowhere else to go. School at least seemed normal.

"On second thought, I'll go."

Len patted my hand. She'd just subtly talked me into going. Mom would have just pushed me out the door and said, "Tough luck." Len was much sneakier. I'd have to watch myself.

Valex rushed in holding his briefcase and kissed Len on the cheek. "Got to go."

The way Len looked at him reminded me of the way my mom looked at my dad—like they were the only two people in the room. Len offered him a plate. "Aren't you going to eat breakfast first?"

He checked the wallscreen. "I have a meeting first thing."

Len held the sappy sauce container over the soycakes and a little of the syrup dripped out. "Please? For Jenny? It's her first day of school."

Boy, was she good.

Valex glanced at me and smiled. "Oh, all right. I can be a few minutes late." He took a seat next to me and picked up a clean spork. This is where he differed from my dad. A few minutes late to my dad would have been like the end of the world. But Valex didn't seem to mind.

He'd be late for me.

I felt special for the first time in a long time. I didn't deserve this attention. "You don't have to."

"I want to." He punched me in the arm. "First day of school, huh? Show them what you've got."

I wasn't sure what I'd show them, but one thing was for certain—they wouldn't see my fear. High-school kids ate fear like gummy worms. My stomach ached. Either I'd eaten too many soycakes, or the nerves were already getting to me.

Better change the subject. "So, what do you do for work?" With the clothes they wore today, he could have been a tight-rope walker for all I knew.

Valex patted his face with a napkin. "I'm a lawyer."

Melancholy pinged inside me. "Really? My dad was a lawyer."

He smiled with pride. "I know. I work in his law firm. The Streetwaters have passed it down from generation to generation. That's one of the reasons why it's an honor to meet you—the daughter of the man who started it all."

"Wow." I thought back to my dad's dreams for his business to continue into the future. He may have been a bit of a workaholic, but his vision had survived the test of time. I was so proud of him.

Len stacked the used plates for C-7 to load in the dishwasher. "I've laid out some clothes on the couch. My older sister, Istell, has a daughter who's just left for the high-rise academies. She said you could have all of her school clothes."

"Do they look anything like what Pell's wearing?"

Len laughed. "Some of them do, but it will be much better than wearing your own clothes. Think about what a pilgrim would look like walking around in your old school."

I smiled despite my gloomy mood. "I'd probably think she was there as part of a historical reenactment during assembly time or a play."

"Exactly. You want to fit in, yes?"

I stuffed a bite of green soycake in my mouth. It tasted like a spinach wafer with white sugar to help it go down. I swallowed hard. "I guess."

"There's not much we can do about secrecy. Word gets around, and I'm sure the other kids can guess who you are, but at least you'll look normal."

I thought of the Barbie cheerleaders and Chad. Nothing could be as bad as they were. "It's okay. I can take some teasing."

Len leaned across the table and took my hand. I froze, putting up a wall to block out all the emotion waiting to burst me into tears. "I want you to be able to make friends. You have a new life ahead of you. Seize the day."

"*Carpe diem*." Pell announced beside me.

I gave her a stare. Since when did seven-year-olds speak Latin?

Len smiled. "That's right. Now let's give Jenny some time to pick an outfit, then off to the hoverbus you two will go."

Panic inched up my spine. "You mean you're not going with us?"

Len looked directly at me, as if I was the seven-year-old. "It's only down the hall and on the platform. Don't worry, Pell will show you the way. And once you get to school, the counselors will be available if you have any questions." She stacked up the dirty dishes on the countertop. "I have a presentation at work today. I have to go in early."

I sighed. Just like my mom. Some things never changed.

I finished most of the soycakes, thinking I'd be the most nutritious teenager on the face of the Earth, then I remembered that everyone ate this way. Geez.

I'd give my right leg for a plate of scrambled eggs and hash browns. Oh, and ketchup. Yeah, ketchup would be perfect. I imagined turning over the bottle, or squeezing out one of those fast-food packets. Shaking, my head, I stopped fantasizing. I had a hideous outfit to pick.

C-7 stood by the couch like a butler, rubbing a cloth over the glass countertop. His robotic fingers clinked eerily against the glass. "Good morning, Jennifer."

I made sure to circle way around him, thinking of all the cyborg movies I'd seen where they went crazy and attacked people, taking over the world.

"Hey there, C-7." I gave him the evil eye, trying to see if he'd react, but he returned to his dusting.

"Good luck at school today."

"Thanks." I looked over the outfits, flipping over a few silver triangle dresses that looked more suitable for microwaving leftovers than wearing to school. I settled for a royal-blue tunic with a gold belt. Sure, I'd look like some futuristic Roman god, but at least the blue would bring out my eyes.

I slipped into the bathroom to change, wondering how to lock a door that dissolved with the press of a panel. *Oh well. Let's hope C-7 doesn't decide to take over the world while I'm in my undies.*

The futuristic shower looked like a torture machine, so I decided to fool with that when I got home. Enough new things for one morning. I kicked off my PJs and slid on a pair of clean, futuristic undies and the tunic. The fabric felt soft and light on my body, instantly regulating my skin temperature. The tunic was more comfortable than it looked. Smoothing out my hair, I decided I looked presentable enough.

Pell waited for me in the living room, typing on a miniscreen. Looking over her shoulder, I saw a bunch of trapezoids with algebra. Super. What would I have to do today? Rocket science?

I sighed, anxiety creeping up my legs, giving me that bubbly-nervous feeling in my stomach. What did it matter? These weren't my friends at my school. Okay, so it was my school, but no one that I knew still went there. Who cared what these futuristic teens thought of me?

An alarm went off on Pell's miniscreen, and she shut the lid and looked up at me. "Time to go."

We walked to the front door panel and Len gave Pell a kiss on the cheek. "Show them how much you've been studying over the summer."

"I will." Pell beamed and grabbed her lunch container.

Len turned to me. "Your parents would be proud of you." She squeezed my shoulder and handed me a lunch container and a miniscreen. It was strange to have Len make me breakfast and see me off to school. Mom always rose at the crack of dawn and left before I'd even gotten up. In a way, I missed Mom's workaholic lifestyle. All this attention made me feel like I was five years old again.

Pell pressed the door panel and the particles dissolved to a chaotic corridor with kids of all ages rushing to school and men and women commuting to work. Pell took my hand and led me through the crowd to a dock where a hoverbus picked us up.

We sat beside a businesswoman clicking on her miniscreen and talking to an input device in her ear.

"Your stop comes after mine." Pell instructed me with her little legs dangling and kicking the seat in front of us. "Watch the screen for Ridgewood Prep. Exit fifty-seven."

She plugged her ear device into her miniscreen and typed away, her little fingers flying over the keypad so fast they blurred. I gazed out the window at the metropolis sprawling out before us, a sea of skyscrapers so close you could jump from one to the next. Hovercars sped in zigzags across the sky, and a dense cloud of smog made the sun seem hazy and distant. As we rounded a corner between two high-rises, a crystal-topped skyscraper with vines and leaves growing underneath the glass came into view.

"That's a greenhouse." Pell nudged my arm and pointed to a series of buildings on the right. "My stop's the next one."

The screen by the driver flashed *Elementary Academy of New England*. The hoverbus stopped and Pell jumped out of her seat. "Good luck today, sillybot." She pecked my cheek with a kiss and jogged down the aisle.

As much as I joked about her being my bodyguard earlier, when the hoverbus took off again, I missed her. It was the first time I was completely alone in this new world.

CHAPTER TEN

The Hotter Chad

I stepped off the hoverbus onto a platform full of perfect-looking high-school models. It was like someone had thrown me into a movie with actors all in their twenties playing well-developed and self-assured teens.

No one had a zit. No one.

Where was the geek squad with the thick glasses? The band nerds with their saxophones and flutes strapped to their backs? The tall, gangly kids with braces?

Ridgewood Prep had turned into *Buffy* meets *Gossip Girl*.

I remembered Len saying it was the best school in New England. Even when I went to it hundreds of years ago, the price tag was staggering enough to think twice. I couldn't imagine what it was today. I was looking at all of the richest kids in New England. Did they have bioengineered features, enhancements to make them see perfectly and have their teeth grow straight?

I followed the crowd, feeling like the smallest, dorkiest has-been the world had ever known. The bell rang and I checked my mini-screen for my schedule, my fingers fumbling over the keypad.

Period 1: Homeroom 504D.

Okay, homeroom. I could deal with that.

I followed the classrooms until I reached 504D and stepped in. Of course, I was majorly late. Everyone stared at me as I walked in, even the teacher. You'd think I'd grown two heads.

"Jenny Streetwater?" The teacher finally found her voice after a long, awkward silence.

"Yes."

"Third screen on the right. Aisle two. I'm Mrs. Rickard."

Everyone sat behind what looked like large, sideways TV screens. What happened to desks? An unoccupied screen sat between a girl that looked like she'd win Miss Universe and a guy who looked so familiar I almost lost my half-digested soycakes on the floor.

Chad?

It couldn't be. He'd be over three hundred years old. My heart leaped up to my throat. Was he frozen, too?

As I rounded the corner of screens, I got a better look. My stomach pitched. This guy wasn't Chad. Although he had Chad's features, he was way hotter, like times one hundred to infinity squared. His features were sharper and more proportional, his body was more muscular, and his hair shone like black midnight, smooth and silky to the point I wanted to run my hands through it.

"Look, it's Neanderthal girl," Miss Universe announced.

I took my seat behind her and in front of the hotter Chad.

Snickers and giggles filled the room, making my cheeks blaze. I slumped forward until my pale hair covered my face.

"Enough, Exara." Mrs. Rickard pressed a panel and a screen flashed on behind her. "Principal Hall has something for all of you to hear."

An older man with gray streaks in his hair, wearing a golden tunic with a fake tie embroidered on the front, held up a miniscreen. "Welcome to another great year at Ridgewood Prep. As you embark on your individual learning journeys, keep your goals in mind at all times and persevere against adversity."

My brain glazed over with all the generalizations. Yadda yadda. Sounded like he was giving a graduation speech, and we hadn't even started classes.

Someone tapped my shoulder, and I turned around to face the better-looking Chad.

He leaned in, dark eyes gleaming. "Are you really from the past?"

I paused, not knowing if he was interested or if he would tease me like Miss Universe. I decided to play it safe. "Yeah."

The principal still gabbed in the background. I cast a glance over to make sure the teacher hadn't noticed me talking. "Why?"

He shrugged. "Just cuz. I think history's cybertopic."

"Cyberwhat?"

"Jennifer, is there something you want to share with the class?"

I whirled around. The first day and I'd already gotten into trouble. "I'm sorry. No, ma'am."

Exara whispered under her breath, "No, *ma'am*? What is this? The Plymouth Mayflower?"

Mrs. Rickard gave Exara a cold stare and then returned to me. "Good." She pressed a panel on the wall and the principal's announcements resumed.

"Psst."

I couldn't believe it. Hotter Chad wanted to get me in trouble again. I steeled myself and pretended not to hear him.

"Jennifer." My name sounded odd on his tongue, like he hadn't said the name Jennifer before. It caught my attention. I eyed Mrs. Rickard and turned around slowly. "What is it?"

"What year?"

I shook my head in confusion.

"What year are you from?"

A light tinkling of music came on the intercom and everyone jumped up from their screen desks. Everyone except for me and Chad's look-alike.

"Two-thousand-twelve."

"Wow." He shook his head like he didn't believe it and gawked as if I'd just won the lottery. "What kind of car did you have?"

"A pink Lexus." I pushed down a wave of homesickness. Even though I'd grabbed his attention, it made me feel like a circus freak.

"No horse and buggy, heh?" Exara shot back from in front of us, holding her miniscreen up to her very large breasts.

Hotter Chad ignored her. "Did it run on gas or diesel?"

"Gas. 35 miles per gallon."

"Per gallon...that's right! They had gallons back then. Was it a Lexus HS?"

I stared at him. "How did you know that?"

"Maxim's a history whiz." Exara pushed her way between us.

"Maxim?" It was hard not to call him Chad.

He stuck his hand past Exara's curvy waist, offering it to me. "Yup. Nice to meet you."

Before I could reach for his hand, Exara moved in front of it. "Come on. Let's get to class, hon."

Maxim glanced at me. "Gotta go." He linked his arm in hers and they walked out together. I stood there and stared with my mouth so far open that a frog could have jumped in. If one still existed.

What had I gotten myself into? It was the first day and I'd already fallen for the beauty queen's boyfriend. There was a big box of "sucker" with my name on it.

"Jennifer, is everything all right?" Mrs. Rickard called to me from over the screendesks. I realized I was the only one left besides her.

"Yeah, I just don't know where I'm going." I fumbled with my miniscreen, not even remembering how to turn it on.

"Press the button on the upper right side."

"Oh yeah."

My schedule popped up like some chart on a video game. Period 2 was General Relativity and Cosmology. That was Einstein stuff, right? I knew about him. I could do this. Stumbling out of home-room, I found my next classroom in less time and wasn't as embarrassingly late. In fact, a few others trickled in after me as light techno music signaled the beginning of class.

I clicked on my miniscreen, proud to remember how. A younger man, maybe in his forties, with a few gray hairs on his head stepped in front of the main screen.

"Click your screens to page twenty-three in your text."

Everyone's fingers flicked over their screendesks. I ran my hands over my screendesk and nothing happened.

The boy next to me whispered, "Plug your miniscreen in, bothead."

"Oh yeah." I acted like I'd just forgotten and reached for the thin wire by my feet. He watched me with a suspicious glare as I ran my fingers along the side to figure out where to put the plug in. The teacher, to my utter embarrassment, came over and plugged my miniscreen in for me. He gave me a wink as if someone had already told him I was a hopeless prospect from the past. I sank into my chair, feeling like a kindergartener in a high-school class.

"This is a review of special relativity and the motivation for considering gravity in terms of curvature of spacetime."

What? He hadn't even introduced himself and he was talking about how spacetime curved. My brain just short-circuited.

The teacher didn't seem to care. He kept babbling nonsense. "Through Riemannian geometry, general relativity, and Einstein's equations, we'll explore an application of general relativity in the study of black holes, gravitational waves, cosmology, as well as recent results on inflation and quantum gravity."

Cosmology? Wasn't that beauty school?

While the others in the class began typing furiously on their screendesks, I sat back and thought about Angela at old Ridgewood Prep. She made faces at me from across the room if the teacher said anything we didn't understand. I missed her so much that my chest hurt and my stomach felt like I'd eaten battery acid.

As period two ended, I was already overwhelmed.

CHAPTER ELEVEN

Others

All I wanted to do in the cafeteria was sink into the sludge in my lunch container and hide for another three hundred years. Too bad the odds of that happening were almost as slim as me waking up from a bad dream. They'd assigned me a "buddy" to show me around the lunchroom, but she disappeared once she found her friends.

Some welcome.

"Hey, Jennifer." Maxim sat across from me, whipping out a container that held a soy sausage. He bit into the end. "Whatcha got?"

I opened my container, afraid to say my adopted mom made my lunch for me. I might as well have dressed like Tiny Tim and begged for friends. "Looks like some green goo, yellow fuzz, and pink water."

He laughed. "That's strawberry kiwi mineral water. My mom buys it all the time."

"Yeah, but what's the rest of this?" I held up the container so the green goo slopped down the other side.

"Hmmmm…looks like veggie mix. The yellow stuff is probably banana-flavored protein pudding."

"Oh." I took out my spork, opened the lid, and swished it around in the sludge.

"Different from a turkey sandwich, huh?"

My eyes flicked up. Finally, someone spoke English. "I used to eat turkey sandwiches all the time. They're my favorite."

"Really?" He looked genuinely interested, which made me feel more at home than I had all day.

I laughed, noticing how his tunic shirt molded to his upper biceps. "Yeah, with mayo."

"Mayonnaise. I bet it tasted cyberlicious." His eyes sparkled with envy. The expression looked good on him. So far, every expression did.

"Better than the leprechaun pancakes I had for breakfast."

"You didn't coat them in sappy sauce?"

I shook my head, feeling ashamed. Pell had even offered me an extra helping. "No."

"Cyberhell, Jennifer. You're missing out. Next time, go for the sappy sauce all the way."

I nodded seriously and smiled at the same time. "Got it." Was I flirting? I certainly hoped not. I couldn't even keep track of my own skyscraper, never mind stalk a new crush. Plus, Angela wasn't here to bounce ideas off of. I couldn't daydream about guys without her.

"Talking to Rip Van Winkle?" Exara slid into a seat beside Maxim and gave me a cruel smile. "Where's your beard?"

"I shaved it off, along with the hair on my back." I stuck my spork into the sludge, pretending it was her face.

Her beautiful features twisted in disgust and Maxim laughed. "Jennifer ate real turkey sandwiches."

"I bet she stepped in real animal poo, too."

Maxim stared at me with interest. "Did you?"

I shrugged. "I had a horse named Thunderbolt. I used to ride every day after school." I smacked myself in the face in my mind. Why did I just say that? It would only give Exara more material to pick on me with.

"A horse? That's so last century." Exara turned to Maxim. "Come on, let's talk about something interesting. Current. Like the annual Autumn Ball." She twirled the fabric of his tunic around her index finger. "What should we dress like this year?"

Maxim shrugged noncommittally. "I don't know. Maybe green like Jennifer's lunch."

Exara clearly didn't appreciate the reference to me. She sniffed her perfect button nose and turned directly toward him, leaving me out of the conversation. I couldn't hear what she whispered to him or his answer.

After another five minutes of eating sludge and being ignored, lunch was over, at least for me. I slipped the smaller containers back into the large one, making sure I didn't forget the spork, even though it was plastic. It didn't look like they threw anything away here. There weren't any garbage cans, only small circular openings in the middle of the tables. I wasn't about to break the recycling chute rules on my very first day by stuffing something illegal down one. Len would just have to sort out my lunch when I got back home.

"Leaving so soon?" Maxim glanced up from his conversation with Exara.

"Yeah, I've got a lot of studying to do." That was a blatant lie. I had no idea what any of my classes were about, except art, and even that one was a little strange with everything done digitally and no paint. Think about it—art with no paint. That was like kindergarten with no glue.

"Take it easy. See you tomorrow in homeroom." He smiled.

My heart melted. I scooped it up off the floor, trying to keep some amount of dignity. "Yeah, see ya."

Exara ran her hand through Maxim's hair, messing it up, temporarily, before it fell back into a perfect swirl. "I'll ask my great-grandma if she wants a friend. You two can live it up, talking about horses and turkey sandwiches." Each syllable came out awkward on her tongue, like me saying *Plymouth Plantation* and *breeches*.

I narrowed my eyes. "Thanks, Exara. You're too kind."

She batted her enormously long black eyelashes, which had to be implants. "I do my best."

I walked away steaming. It was only en route to my next class I realized that Exara had just given me the best idea I'd had since I woke up.

What if there were others like me?

People frozen around 2012 and awoken this year.

My cancer wasn't all that uncommon, and the chances of someone else being healed from the same thing when the cure came out had to be pretty good. At least I'd have a friend who understood what I was going through.

I zombied through the rest of the day, waiting for the moment I could get home and do a wallscreen search on my own. *Sorry, Angela. No one can ever replace you.* But Ridgewood Prep was worse than World War IV, and I needed to find a substitute best friend.

When the final set of techno music played, signaling the end of school, relief washed over me. I'd gotten through my first day with my ego bruised, but alive. The hoverbus hung on the same platform where it had dropped me off, and I boarded it, taking a seat in the back by myself.

I watched for Pell's stop, eager to see her again. The hoverbus came to a halt, and an older woman got on. No Pell. Panic rose, crushing my chest and throat. What if I'd taken the wrong bus? What if I couldn't find my way back home?

The older woman took the seat next to mine, and I nudged her arm to get her attention. She gave me a tired, uninterested look in return.

"Where are all the kids?"

Her hair had gray roots, and her tunic was frayed at the edges. I wondered what job she had at Pell's school. "They got out an hour earlier."

"Oh, I see." I slumped back in my seat in embarrassment and relief. Pell was probably at home eating more of that sappy sauce. I didn't have a bodyguard, but I could make it back if I could remember my building number.

The greenhouse we'd passed that morning flew by. The hoverbus was close. I sat on the edge of my seat, annoying the woman as I leaned over her to get a decent view of the buildings. Each one looked the same, a glassy front scattered with ledges for hovercrafts.

The platform where Pell and I had boarded jutted out with a familiar stripe of yellow and orange and I knew I was home free. Building 221863, section FFgGA. Okay. That would take some time to remember. For now I could get by on looks alone.

I buzzed the door to Valex and Len's apartment, and the sides parted to reveal C-7 wearing an apron on his metal frame. "Hello, Jennifer."

"Where are Valex and Len?"

"Your adoptive parents remain at work. They will return home at five forty-five and six fifteen respectively. I hope you had a nice day at school."

"It was awful." I snuck by him, careful not to brush up against his metal arms. Just thinking about touching him gave me the willies.

Pell jumped up from the couch. "Yay! My new big sis is home." She ran around the living room to C-7 and stuck her tongue out. "I don't need you anymore."

"Very true, Pell."

For a millisecond I felt bad for the robot as he lumbered to the kitchen, where I smelled more soyfood cooking.

"He cooks, too?"

"He does everything a human can, just not as good." Pell muttered under her breath, watching him slink away. She took my hand. "Come on, I want to play more Pixie Swap."

"Wait a second. I need you to help me with something first."

She stared at me, almost pouting like nothing could be more important than Pixie Swap. "What is it?"

"I need to find some information on the Internet...is that what you still call it?"

"You mean the cybernet, bothead. Find out about what?"

"If there are people like me, people who woke up after a very long time."

"Oh, all right." Pell stomped over to the wallscreen and clicked it on. Her fingers flew over the buttons. I tried to pay attention, but she typed too fast. A search engine came up with a blinking cursor.

She looked over her shoulder. "What do you want me to say?"

"Search for cryogenic sleep subjects."

Twenty minutes and several searches later, Pell huffed in frustration. All of her searches had ended up with blank blue pages. "I can't do it. Nothing comes up."

"Is there any other way?"

She shrugged. "You could ask C-7. He's not supposed to use the cybernet, but he did once for me when I needed to find my dad's miniscreen number."

I glanced over my shoulder as he banged around in the kitchen. "I'm not sure I want his help."

She shrugged. "Whatever. Let's go play Pixie Swap."

As much as I enjoyed watching a little kid kick my butt at math, I needed that information. "Hold on a minute."

I walked into the kitchen just as C-7 turned on some sort of food processor, churning an orange liquid.

When he saw me come in, he pressed the button and the machine's buzzing trailed off. "Jennifer, can I help you?"

I'd work my way up to asking him to break the rules to help me snoop around. "What's for dinner?"

"Soyloaf with orange marmalade sauce."

My stomach gurgled in protest. "Oh. When will it be ready?"

His head clicked as he tilted it. "Six thirty-four."

"After Valex and Len get home?"

"Correct."

The wallscreen read four-thirty. That gave me plenty of time for fishing. I stuck my hands on my sides, looking for pockets in my tunic that weren't there. Awkwardly, I settled for leaning on the counter. "I was wondering if you could help me find something."

"I am always at your service, Jennifer."

"Great." Also kind of stalkerish. I let that slip. I needed his help. "I'd like to find others like me, you know, people from my generation woken up hundreds of years later."

Little gears in C-7's neck turned like he was thinking. Did robots think? No, they computed. He must have been computing.

C-7 froze as if he'd come to a conclusion. "I am not allowed to use the cybernet to access information."

"I know. Pell told me. But, I was thinking, just this once? I really need to find others like me. I feel so alone."

C-7's eyes stared, boring into me. How could a robot understand how it felt to be alone? Besides that, he wouldn't even play Pixie Swap with Pell because it was *beyond his programming*.

I turned away, feeling sheepish for even asking. "Never mind."

"The only subject I can find in our geographical area is Martha Maynard."

"What?"

"She was born in nineteen-ninety-six, frozen in twenty-twenty, and awoken sixty-seven years ago."

"You mean you searched from your head?"

"My central processor can connect wirelessly to the computer mainframe of this household."

I shook my head, trying to absorb all the information. There was someone else like me, someone born in the nineteen-hundreds. Nineteen-ninety-six, to be exact—that would make her about my age. Except she lived longer than me by eight years, putting her in her twenties when she was frozen. My head wrapped around the math, making me yearn for Pixie Swap level three.

"You mean to tell me she's around eighty years old?" I might as well go meet Exara's great-grandmother.

"Yes, but she had a similar experience to yours, making her an adequate product of my search."

"Is there anyone closer to my age?"

C-7 shook his head. "There are subjects awoken in their teens, but they were frozen many years later than you. The next closest patient is Cindy Lewis, born in twenty-thirty-four, frozen in twenty-forty-seven, and awoken in twenty-one-eighty-nine. Subject is no longer living and would, therefore, not prove useful to your purposes. Other subjects frozen around the same time as you didn't survive or were awoken much earlier. Some, I'm afraid, are still in cryosleep, waiting for the doctors to find a cure."

"Right." Shivers went down my spine as I thought of those poor frozen people. Maybe I was lucky the doctors woke me up after all.

"My apologies, Jennifer." Could C-7 feel my disappointment, my heartbreak? It certainly seemed like it.

"Don't worry about it, C-7."

The robot resumed work with the food processer, and the buzzing rang in my ears. All I wanted was to watch those videos of my previous life, but Pell waited for me. I'd have to settle for fairies on lily pads and equations that made my brain hurt.

CHAPTER TWELVE

Special

Exara's screendesk lay empty. Secretly, I celebrated, plunking down at the screendesk behind hers. Guilt came next, and I halted the party before it raged out of control. What if she was deathly ill? Or even worse, what if she had to be frozen like me? Even though I already hated her, I didn't wish my fate on anyone.

"Morning, Jennifer." Maxim whispered from behind as he took his seat.

"Hey Maxim." I tried to look cool and calm while my heart raced in his presence. "Is Exara sick?"

"Exara never gets sick." He wore a sea-green tunic today, the color bringing out flecks in his eyes. "Her personal dietician makes her take a regimen of vitamins. Her immune system is hyperstrong."

Oh, excuse me. Was she so special she could cut class whenever she wanted? "Where is she?"

"She's at her bi-monthly beauty treatment."

"What? Did an eyelash accidentally fall out?"

Maxim laughed. "You're funny. No. Her eyelash didn't fall out. She gets a facial, teeth whitening and straightening, color enhancement for her skin, hair, and eyes, and any accumulated fat cells burnt off, among other things."

I shook my head. "All that, huh?"

He nodded like it was a nail appointment. "Life in the upper levels isn't what it used to be. Finding a decent career is getting more and more competitive. You need every advantage you can have to get ahead and stand out." It was the first time I saw something close to anxiety in his eyes. "Even how you look is important, right down to every eyelash."

"Well, I'm doomed." I turned around in my seat, shaking my head. Did he buy into all that crap? If so, I didn't want anything more to do with him. I tried to focus on the morning announcements, but Maxim wouldn't drop it.

As our homeroom teacher talked about planning for the Autumn Ball festivities, Maxim's voice hissed behind me, "What do you mean, doomed?"

I turned around. "My bottom row of teeth is so crooked that it looks like some little mouth-gnome kicked them all in. My eyelashes are nonexistent, and I can't even understand the first General Relativity class."

I stopped, my mouth hanging open. Why was I telling him this? I almost died. I'd just vomited all my insecurities to the hottest guy in school.

"You don't need all those extra enhancements." Maxim leaned forward. "You're special, Jennifer."

Was I hallucinating due to too much sappy sauce? I had tried more than usual at Pell's insistence. "Special? Because I'm over three hundred years old?"

"No, because you don't look like anyone here." His hand rose up and touched my hair, spreading it out in a veil. The falling hair tickled the side of my face and my scalp tingled. "No one has hair this color. It reminds me of sunlight in the morning on a day when all the smog has blown away."

I froze, utterly speechless. *What do you say when a gorgeous guy recites something like poetry just for you? Am I hearing things as well?* He did have a point. Back in 2012, most of the people in Maine were Caucasian and pale. Now the population in the formerly backwoods state looked more like Boston, with a wide array of ethnicities.

The techno bell rang as it always did—at the most inconvenient moment—and everyone shot up from their desks. Maxim shouldered his backpack and his tone turned trivial, like we'd just talked about last night's homework assignment. "Besides, I can help you with that Einstein business. See you at lunch."

I couldn't wait until lunch. General Relativity dragged by as if time had stopped. I knew what that felt like, right? The guy that had called me bothead fell asleep on his screendesk, drooling, and I found a way to scribble concentric circles with my fingernail on the sides of the screen and erase them when the teacher walked by. Some of the concepts were actually pretty neat—our universe was still expanding, which would mean endless possibilities for other signs of life. Aliens. Although I'd joked about it with Mom and Timmy, I wished I'd been woken up when there were aliens. Anything would be better than Exara.

Just when I thought I'd die of waiting, the techno jingle rang and I filed into the lunchroom. Maxim sat in the same spot as yesterday. He smiled, his perfect white teeth gleaming. He even had a chin dent.

I wanted to kiss it. Wasn't like I'd kissed anything in my life besides stuffed animals and Timmy's cheek.

"Get through General Relativity okay?"

I sat across from him and took out my lunch container, this time packed by C-7 because Len was running late. "Yeah. It was interesting today."

"Good. See. You'll adjust to life here just fine. You just have to give us a chance."

I pulled out a container of some gelatinous blue stuff that jiggled. "Jenny. That's what my friends call me."

"Jenny. I like the sound of that."

I sporked the Smurf food and stuffed it in my mouth. The spoonful wiggled on my tongue, tasting like mint. "It's the plainest name in all of America."

"Nowadays, with names like XoXo and Shizznizz, it's one of a kind."

I covered my mouth to stop my slimy food from spewing all over the lunch table. "Shizznizz? Really?"

"Yeah." He pointed across the cafeteria. "See that guy over there, the one with the orange hair?"

I scanned the table across the room. A guy leaned back in his seat, banging his spork on the table and listening to some jack in his ear. "Yeah."

"Shizznizz O'Riley. I'm not kidding ya."

"Jeez. What were his parents thinking?"

"Only that he'd be the mega-coolest guy in school."

"Well, they were clearly wrong."

Maxim stopped mid-bite. "What do you mean?"

"'Cuz *you're* the mega-coolest guy in school." I tsk-tsked and shook my head. "They should have named him Maxim." Although I sounded sarcastic, I meant it. I pretended to drop my spork in my lap to hide the blush on my face. Why did I always gush like a baby when I was nervous?

Thankfully, he didn't freak out. Instead he waved my compliment away like he didn't deserve it. "You won't think so when you see me dance."

"You can't be that bad."

"Trust me. I am."

The techno bell rang too soon, mocking me with its casual tone. I could have stayed in that lunchroom for the rest of the day talking about dancing, names, and General Relativity as it applied to me and Maxim. Ironically, for a three-hundred-year-old teen, time had run out. Tomorrow Exara would be back, and I'd turn back into the third wheel.

"See ya." I picked up my backpack as he stuffed his lunch container into his.

He reached in the front pocket and passed a plastic card across the table. Did they allow teens to have credit cards nowadays? "Here's my miniscreen number. Call me if you have any questions on Einstein."

I took the card, feeling the raised digits under my skin. "Thanks."

"Later, Jenny." His eyes stuck on mine and I couldn't move. Chad's playful eyebrows appeared amongst the sharper features that made him all that much more enticing. I made a mental note to ask C-7 who Maxim's ancestors were.

His lips curled slightly and he spun around, leaving me in the lunchroom with the gurgling of the recycling tubes.

When I got home, Pell was napping while C-7 folded laundry. Since I'd already asked him to investigate the other cryosleepers, I didn't think it was the best time to ask about Maxim. Even robots had their limits.

I dragged my feet to my room and took out Maxim's card, flipping it over and over on my bed. The numbers shimmered in the fluorescent light like the wings of a butterfly.

Why did he want to help me? Was I just another history experiment for him? Or was there something more? Something I'd never had with anyone at Ridgewood Prep.

I needed to talk to Angela so badly, my heart ached. She'd know exactly what his intentions were. I reached for the closest thing to her and popped in the next video in the series I referred to as *My Previous Life*.

Timmy stood in front of the camera holding Buzz Lightyear and his ratty Elmo doll. His hair had grown out into long curls around his ears. He looked like he'd grown two inches. Watching an older Timmy dance around brought a wave of melancholy.

"Hi, Jenny. You're still sleeping. When are you going to wake up?"

He held his Buzz Lightyear figure up and flew him through the air. Buzz collided with Elmo, who, of course, fell on the floor with a *kaboom*.

"Mommy says not to talk about you because it makes her sad. So I decided to turn on the camera and talk to you myself."

In the background, I heard my mom's voice. "Timmy, what are you doing? Lunch is ready."

The sound of her voice cut to my heart, slicing out a piece. I missed her. Even if she *had* ranted on and on about her upcoming campaign. Now I'd sit and listen, maybe even help make signs.

My mom came into Timmy's room and grabbed his hand. She wore the same blouse she'd worn to a New Year's party last year—really three hundred years ago—with black sequins in the front. I decided I missed sequins, too.

"Wait! I have to shut off the video." Timmy ran back into the room and put his little arm up. He stuck his tongue out at the screen and made googly eyes before it flickered off. I laughed and cried at the same time, feeling like he was in the next room when he really was a world away.

Angela appeared on the next clip. I almost gagged when I saw who she sat next to. Chad played on his iPhone, probably texting his best jock buds. They sat in the stadium, watching the cheerleaders practice their routine on the football field.

"Hi, Jenny." She seemed happier than I remembered her, with a squeak in her voice and a bounciness to her curls. "I wanted to bring you along for the preparations for the Autumn Ball. Shelly Smith is working on the theme this year. It's going to be Underwater Illusions. See, the cheerleaders are all dressed in green and blue."

The video focused on the cheerleading team and I sighed, sitting back and fingering Maxim's card. Since when did Angela care about them?

She turned the camera back to her face. Her eyes blinked and she bit the side of her mouth. I knew that expression. She was hiding something. Or was it just my imagination on overdrive? Maybe she tried to hide her sadness for me. I didn't know.

"Chad and I are working on the decorations. We thought we'd do a big disco ball in the center with streamers that blew like currents underwater. What do you think?"

Chad's voice mumbled beside her, "Jenny never liked that kind of stuff, Angie. She's going to think this is the lamest video of all time."

I laughed. He was right.

Wait a second. How come he called her Angie? And how did he know me so well?

I thought he didn't even know my last name. It must have been the famous "after you're dead" syndrome. You know, when someone died tragically and then everyone pretended they knew them just to have something to talk about, because knowing them turned from lame to mega-cool. Maybe I was the famous dead girl at Ridgewood Prep.

But I wasn't dead. They were.

Tears stung my eyes. I clicked off the screen. I'd seen enough for tonight.

CHAPTER THIRTEEN

Window to the Past

The weekend came sooner than I wanted. I hadn't had another chance to talk with Maxim alone, and now I had two whole days off with my substitute family and a robot that still freaked me out. I thought about calling Maxim's miniscreen, but I actually understood General Relativity, so the whole conversation would be a lie. Besides, he was with Exara, and stealing someone's boyfriend wasn't on my moral compass. Even if she was mean. *Not that I could, anyway.*

Instead of pining away for someone I couldn't have, which was the story of my life, I had other things on my mind. After another family breakfast of soycakes, I waited until C-7 was alone, loading the dishwasher. I walked into the kitchen just as he dropped a spork into a utensil holder resting on a tray that came out of the wall. He set each plate a perfect half-inch apart.

"Greetings, Jennifer. Did you enjoy your breakfast?"

"Sure. I'm getting used to those soycakes. You just have to load on a whole lot of sappy sauce."

"Although not nutritionally balanced, the sappy sauce provides an incentive to consume more."

"Um, yeah. Anyway, I was wondering about the conversation we had the other day. About Martha Maynard."

C-7's silver eyes scanned the area behind my head. I leaned in and whispered, "Don't worry, they're all busy in the other room."

"What would you like to know about Martha Maynard?"

I fidgeted with a sticky spork before popping it into the tray. C-7 moved the utensil slightly to the right in perfect formation with the others. I'd watched too many of those cheap sci-fi movies growing up, because crazy robots from the future stuck in my mind. Again. If he wanted to, he had enough power to jam that spork right down my throat.

I blinked and swallowed hard. "I'd like to know where she lives. I want to meet her."

The gears in his neck spun, and I wondered if I'd sent him into hyperdrive.

"If it's too much trouble—"

"Apartment thirty-two AA, high-rise five hundred eighty-four, level seventy-eight."

I stared. *Wake up, Jennifer, and write it down.* I needed a piece of paper. *Wait. They don't have paper any more.* Panicking, I searched for my miniscreen. I was always losing it, and I bet it cost more than a laptop.

"I have downloaded the coordinates, along with directions to her high-rise, to your miniscreen's central processor. Code name: Martha."

"C-7, I don't know what to say."

"Valex and Len plan to take Pell to the recycling factory today for a school assignment. That would be the most opportune time to leave."

Suspicion clouded my thoughts. It all seemed too easy. Maybe Valex and Len were testing me, trying to see what kind of teen I really was. Or what if C-7 wanted me out of the apartment so he could take over the world? "Why are you helping me?"

"I am here to help, Jennifer. It is what I do." His voice sounded so genuine that it almost broke my heart, like a lost puppy. He had to be telling the truth. Suddenly, I worried about him.

"What would Valex and Len do if they knew you helped me?"

"They would erase my memory and have me reprogrammed." He said it so matter-of-factly, almost like he didn't care. "That is why I advise you to remain silent."

I ran my fingers across my lips like a zipper. "My mouth is sealed." Robots were way cooler than I thought. At least this one was.

I pretended to do homework on my miniscreen until Valex rushed into the living room, packing a travel bag with soybean wafers. He looked at me as if I was that lost puppy. For a second, Timmy's eyes stared through time. "Are you sure you don't want to come with us?"

I blinked and Timmy turned back into Valex. "Nah. I have a lot of work to do. These classes are harder than I'm used to."

"Of course. You'll catch up. I know you will." Valex put a hand on my shoulder and squeezed gently. "Let me know if you need any help."

Oh, I already have a stellar tutor. I almost blurted out Maxim's name and decided against it. "I have someone to call."

His eyebrow rose.

"A study partner."

"Wonderful. I'm glad you're making friends." He zipped up the backpack, and Exara came to mind. *And enemies, too.*

Valex threw me a soybean wafer. "You have our miniscreen numbers if you need to reach us."

I pocketed the wafer, thankful for Valex's laid-back attitude in this case. Maybe he didn't care about animals as much as I wanted him to, but he did give me the freedom I needed to accept this world. My dad would have ordered me to come with the family and put in some "family time." Now I wished I'd enjoyed his forced trips more often.

"Jenny, are you okay?" Valex had stopped packing and stared at me. My anguish must have shone on my face.

For a moment, I almost changed my mind. I could use some family time right now. But, I needed answers and this was the only way to get them. I forced a smile. "Yes, I'll be fine. C-7 will keep me company."

Pell ran in and collapsed at my feet. "Jenny, you don't want to stay with bothead, do you?"

I patted the top of her head where her perfect black hair parted. It was getting easier to separate her from Timmy. When I thought about it, she looked nothing like him. That was all from me projecting my loss. "Don't worry about me. I'll be fine. Take good notes on your field trip."

"I will." Pell jumped up. "I'd like to be a plant manager when I grow up."

Most kids I knew wanted to be vets or ballerinas. I had to remind myself animals were extinct. I wondered if they still performed the Nutcracker. It would look pretty silly in those triangular tunics. "That's very practical of you."

Len slipped into the living room and gave me another one of her million-dollar smiles. "Let's go, everyone."

It was almost as if she was trying to broadcast "happy" across the room, but life didn't work that way, no matter how sneaky you were. She'd never be a substitute for my real mom. They said their good-byes and rushed to catch the next hoverbus.

I waited another thirty minutes before I typed MARTHA into my miniscreen and came up with the coordinates. After saying good-bye to C-7, I slipped out the door, followed the GPS on my miniscreen, and found the right landing for the hoverbus. Martha Maynard's high-rise was ten stops away, so I sat in the front, paying attention and counting as each stop passed.

Most of the people using the hoverbus system were decked out with tech gadgets, silky tunics and beauty enhancements, but every now and then I saw a normal-looking person slip through and I wondered how they got along in this harsh, plastic world. No one talked to me, so I kept my mouth shut and observed from the safety of my bus seat.

My heart sped with every passing stop. I was so excited to finally meet someone who'd understand what I was going through. Maybe we could talk about Dunkin' Donuts, grassy meadows, and penguins. Yes, I wanted to talk about penguins and polar bears until my tongue fell out of my mouth.

The hoverbus beeped and I watched the screen, making sure the coordinates matched the ones on my miniscreen. My GPS said to go for it, so I de-boarded onto a platform much like the one at Valex and Len's high-rise.

I stepped over and shivered, pulling my tunic tighter against my body. This building exuded creepiness. The lights weren't as bright, and scuffs, scratches, and dents marked the chrome floor. A few shady teens with neon hair and wearing hooded tunics lurked near the platform, and I passed them without making eye contact. I walked swiftly and kept my eyes on the corridor. *Yeah, I know where I'm going. Don't waste my time.*

The air smelled like oil and burnt circuits, and the walls were bare. No fancy holopaintings with oscillating pictures. Not that I liked them anyway. None of the pictures looked natural, even though they supposedly showed scenes like meadows and oceans. *If you'd walked on the real beach with sand between your toes, you'd see how fake the bright pixels of ocean looked.*

Discolored water stains left haloes on the carpet. Further in, I passed swirly marks that looked a lot like gang symbols. Did they even have gangs in 2314? Fear prickled the hairs on my arms as I took the elevator down to Martha's floor. I wasn't going to let this place scare me. C-7 had piqued my curiosity, and I knew I couldn't go home empty-handed. I'd always wonder what Martha was like.

I buzzed her door and no one answered. Maybe she wasn't home. Where did old ladies go in the future? I pictured her playing bridge at a YMCA, but they wouldn't have real playing decks, would they? The game would probably be on a wallscreen. The thought of old people and technology didn't work in my head. That was *so* my generation. *These old people were probably better at technology than I am.* The irony was that, besides Martha, I was the oldest of them all.

I glanced down the empty corridor, not wanting to have to go all the way back through the stinky halls and wait on the platform for the next hoverbus near the futuristic gang. I buzzed again, and the screen by the door flashed on. A wrinkled face surrounded by bluish-gray hair stared back at me. She growled. "Go away."

"I'm here to see Martha Maynard." My words squeaked out.

Her face turned from a sour pout to a tight-lipped frown. "I'm not expecting any visitors. Get the hell off my doorstep or I'll call the police."

Geez. Now I knew how Dorothy felt when she met the Wicked Witch of the West. I almost melted into a puddle of sludge on the spot. I'd come too far and risked too much to retreat in defeat. Hardening my nerve, I stood on tiptoe so she could get a good look at my face. "My name is Jennifer Streetwater. I was born in nineteen-ninety-five and I've just been awoken from cryosleep. I need to talk to you."

Her watery eyes widened like I was the Ghost of Christmas Past. She turned her head and something beeped. The screen flashed off. *That's it. End of the road. I scared her away.*

I kicked the wall behind me and turned to leave. The doors to her apartment buzzed and parted, and she stood, wearing a frilly apron, with a china teacup in her hand and a *real silver spoon* in the other. "Don't just stand there looking like a lost kitten. Come in."

All of a sudden I questioned *her* motives. Would she ransom me to poor Valex and Len or sell me to those neon-haired dudes hanging outside? *She's just a little old lady. Honestly, Jennifer, you've come all the way down here and you can't step two feet in the door?*

I wanted to know so much about her—what happened in her life here, who she'd been before, how she got that silver spoon. Curiosity drove me forward and I stepped inside. The doors automatically closed behind me.

"Earl Grey, black, or mint?"

"What?" A black cat pranced around the corner, rubbing up against the wall. It seemed so normal to me, but an alarm went off inside my head. Animals were supposed to be extinct.

"What kind of tea do you want?"

"Ummmm. Whatever you're having." I stared at the cat as the fuzzball pranced toward me and hissed. Its eyes glowed yellow in the dim light. *No way it's mechanical.*

"Leave her alone, Jumbo. She's all right." Martha poured me a steaming cup of tea. In my opinion, tea was discolored, dirty water. I needed answers, though, so I accepted the steaming cup and took a seat on her real cotton couch. After all the plastic cups I'd drunk out of since I woke up, the china felt natural under my fingers.

I stared at Jumbo. "How did—how is it possible?"

"DNA cloning." Martha spoke as if about what kind of tea she'd given me.

"I thought animals were extinct."

"If you have enough money, they can do anything." She sat beside me on the couch and Jumbo rubbed up against her legs. "You can see where I've spent my savings."

My hand itched to touch him, but I knew from Angela's cat that not all of the furry friends let strangers come close. I still had a scar on the back of my hand after all these years. "Money well spent."

She assessed me up and down, almost as if still trying to decide if I was the real deal, or if I'd lied to get free tea. "Only a true cryosleeper from my time would say that."

"Well, that's what I am, whether I like it or not."

She sipped her tea with a slurp. "Most people would argue animals take resources that should be allotted to a human. How can you feed a cat when so many humans are starving below?"

"Below where?"

"In the lower levels, of course."

The lower levels had been alluded to but never directly mentioned until now. It was like everyone lived in denial of some underlying disease. To think that everyone lived high up in skyscrapers and attended Ridgewood Prep was like wearing rainbow glasses all the time. How could I have been so naïve?

"Don't worry. You'll learn in time." She glanced at my full teacup and I pretended to sip.

I didn't know how much time I had, so I got right to the point. "Martha, I miss my family and friends. I miss grass and milkshakes, pens and paper, bells that ring before my next class. Is it ever going to get better?"

She sighed, slumping back into the couch. "The pain only dulls over time. It doesn't go away."

"What am I supposed to do?"

"Stop looking back. There's no time-travel machine that can take you where you want to go. Believe me, I've looked into it." Martha stared at me with intensity in her eyes. "All you can do is work to build a better future for yourself. I didn't realize that until it was too late. Now I'm stuck in a cheap apartment with a sixteen-year-old overweight cat."

She grabbed my arm, and I cringed. Her grip was surprisingly strong. "Don't wait until it's too late."

"It's already too late." I pulled away and downed my tea in one gulp. "I wanted to work for National Geographic saving polar bears and African elephants. Now all the animals, besides Jumbo, are extinct, so my dreams are gone."

I picked at the frayed cotton couch. Why was I telling this stranger my deepest thoughts? I shot up, and Jumbo looked at me with curiosity. "I'm sorry. I don't mean to bother you with my problems."

Martha shook her head as if I didn't bother her at all. "There *is* another way."

I dropped back down to the couch, enjoying the familiar smell of mothballs. "What do you mean?"

"Look at Jumbo. There's an environmental group that has stockpiles of the DNA of every single animal that ever existed on Earth, even the dinosaurs. A micro Noah's Ark, all in test tubes instead of livestock stalls."

I thought of rooms full of test tubes marked with labels like "red squirrel," "elk," and "buffalo." It was a door that couldn't be unlocked. Not with the world the way it was. "What good will it do if there's no habitat for them, no food to feed them?" I was rich, but I didn't want to open some rinky-dink zoo where little kids poked penguins with sticks and tigers paced back and forth in front of metal bars.

Martha's eyes traveled across the room. She swished her tea around in her mouth as if deciding what to say next. "This group of people...Well, let's just say they've found a way."

"Found a way how?"

"They look for habitats to bring back extinct species."

"Who are 'they?'" She talked about them as if they were the mafia or FBI. My interest was sparked. Maybe they were. "How do I learn more about them?"

"You can't find them on the cybernet. They're too controversial."

I sighed, frustrated. Was this old lady pulling my leg? Did she have nothing else to do? Looking at Jumbo, I thought not. "So, how do you know about them?"

She placed her teacup down gently on a white doily on the armrest of the couch. Her eyes held a spark of a secret. "I wanted to join them."

"Why didn't you?"

"I was too old. They need young people like you."

"Why?"

She twitched her nose. "You're a curious little girl, aren't you?"

I shrugged, hating being called a girl. I'd had to accept that I was over three hundred years old.

"What I'm about to tell you is a secret. You hear?"

I nodded, wondering if I really wanted to hear what she had to say. Wasn't ignorance bliss?

"The Timesurfers, that's what they're called. They scour the galaxy for planets like Earth, planets where humanity can start anew, where they can bring back all of the extinct species and live in harmony with nature."

"Why do they need young people?"

"Because they don't send out droids. They send real people on their scout ships. It's the only way to be sure, to claim a planet in their name."

"That's impossible. It would take thousands of years to reach the nearest star." I hadn't been paying attention in my General Relativity class for nothing.

"That's why you have to be young, dear. They put you in cryosleep. The computer wakes you once you reach the planet."

The thought of entering cryosleep voluntarily sent shivers throughout my body.

Martha must have noticed my repulsion because she gave me a knowing look. "It's not easy. That's why I waited so long to decide. Too long. I didn't want to be frozen again. It was just too scary after what I'd been through. You know how it is—not knowing when you'll wake up. If you'll wake up."

Martha shivered as if she was cold, then shrugged it off. "I thought I could adapt to this lifestyle and I gave it a good try. But, with my rudimentary education—by their standards, mind you—because I have a degree in Art History, all I could get was a job in a recycling plant, sorting garbage. I tried to move up, but someone younger and faster always beat me to it.

"When I finally approached the Timesurfers, they said I was too old. So, I saved up for Jumbo for years—he was my dream. Finally, I had enough to make that dream a reality. Now I sit here and watch the wallscreen, pet my kitty, and wait for my life to end."

The desolation of her situation weighed me down, as if I had boulders rubbing against each other in my heart. "Martha, I'm so sorry."

"Don't feel bad for me." Martha took my teacup and brought hers and mine into the kitchen. She pressed a panel and the dishwasher came out of the wall. "I lived my life. I made my choices. Learn from my mistakes. If there's one thing you'll find out, it's that none of us have much time."

My miniscreen beeped. I clicked the lid open and a message flashed on. *Valex and Len will be home in one hour.*

C-7 was on the ball. I flipped the lid down before Martha reentered the room. "Thank you for your time."

"You're not going to stay? I have another pot of tea brewing."

My stomach clenched. The first cup was enough. "I have to go, but I'll come back and visit, if you don't mind."

Her eyes sparkled with hope before she blinked it away. "Why visit an old crone like me?"

"Because we have something in common, something no one else on Earth has." I walked up and gave her a hug before turning toward the door. She smelled like mothballs and lilac perfume, just like a normal grandma from 2012. I soaked it in. "See you next time."

I turned to leave so she couldn't see the tears welling in my eyes. The door sensed my presence and opened automatically. I walked into the hallway, smelling oil and burnt circuits again. It was like I'd taken a time machine back to my world and stepped into the future once again. It crushed me to leave.

"Bye, Jennifer." The sides of her door closed behind me before I realized she had remembered my name.

CHAPTER FOURTEEN

Confession

I rushed back to my high-rise, afraid Valex and Len would arrive before I got back. If they did, I'd have to answer a slew of questions, and C-7 would be in trouble. He'd put himself out on a limb for me, and I still had no idea why. Whatever the case, I didn't want his memory erased. What if we got one of those crazy, world-domination robots in his place?

The hoverbus sped towards my high-rise, and I watched the GPS on my miniscreen to be certain I didn't miss the stop. People took so long to get on and off at each stop, I almost stood up and shouted at them to hurry up. When the driver reached my platform, I stood by the door, ready to go. He gave me a suspicious look while I bounced on tiptoe.

I shrugged. "Gotta make curfew." *Hopefully he knows what curfew is.*

The driver pressed a panel and the doors parted. I jumped onto the platform and rushed to my level, pushing by anyone who got in my way. I buzzed the door with shaky fingers, feeling so guilty at skipping out, I was sure my face was as red as the multiplication pixie in Pell's game.

C-7 flashed on the screen. Did his eyes blink in relief, or was it my imagination? "Prompt arrival, Jennifer." The door opened and I scurried inside. Plopping down on the plastic couch, I finally breathed.

Gears turned as C-7 walked over and stood before me. "Did you find everything you were looking for?"

"I did. Thank you for giving me the information." I closed my eyes, trying to block out the world.

"If you truly found everything, why do you seem so sad?"

I sighed, opening my eyes slowly. No rest for me. You'd think I wouldn't need it after all those years spent sleeping, but my body weighed me down and weariness grabbed hold of me. Three hundred years were catching up.

"I miss two-thousand-twelve. In today's world, I'm a freak."

C-7 stood in silence, as if what I said didn't compute.

Why was I telling my problems to a robot? I shook my head and stood up. Talking to Martha had made me tremble with homesickness. I needed to watch those videos, give myself a little normalcy.

"We are all freaks in one way or another." The corners of his mouth turned up. "You have to be who you are."

Philosophy advice, no less, from a computer with a head? "Whatever." I'd had enough lectures for one day. I turned toward my room. "Tell Valex and Len I've gone to bed early."

"What about dinner?"

I showed him the soywafer Valex had given me. "This will do."

"Jennifer, that meal does not meet nutritional standards."

First he gives me advice, and now he's my new cyborg mom?

"Thanks, C-7. I'll try to remember that."

The stack of videos sat in my room like a shrine to the past. I pulled the next one out and popped it into the adapter Valex had connected to the wallscreen. Guilt pinged my gut. Valex had found time to set this up in his busy schedule and I hadn't even thanked him.

Red and blue balloons floated through the air. A podium sat on a stage, and people cheered in the audience. Had someone taped over my precious memories? Rage swelled up until my mom took the stage. She wore a bright pink suit, and a perfect conglomeration of curls covered her head. Flawless rose lipstick highlighted her smile.

She did it. She won the vote for mayor.

Mom started her speech and I turned up the volume. "Dear townspeople, I am extremely honored and humbled to have been voted as your new mayor. I'm excited to accept the responsibilities your vote has entrusted me with. I am endlessly grateful to receive the majority of votes and your empowering confidence in my abilities. I can't wait to start."

The crowd cheered, throwing up programs, roses, and hats. I never felt more proud of my mom.

She took in a deep breath, as if her next words required extra courage. "Many people have helped me along this journey, and I'd like to thank my husband, my son, Timmy, and my dear daughter, Jennifer. We are all waiting for you to wake up, my sleeping beauty, and we all love you."

Mom wiped her eyes and sniffed. I did the same, mirroring her. *I love you, too, Mom.*

For a second she paused, almost as if she heard me and my heart caught in my throat. Could I send a mental message across the years of time? The connection jump-started my hopes. *Mom, can you hear me?*

She blinked, continuing her speech, and the moment was gone. "Without your support, I wouldn't be here today."

The rest of the speech blurred as the tears welled in my eyes. People from all over town came up to congratulate her, then the picture faded to gray static. She couldn't hear me. She was gone. I was looking at an image made from pixels, an image that was not my real mom.

I was so frustrated that I almost turned the video off, but Angela came on the screen, crying almost as hard as I was. I sucked up a sob and listened, more concerned for my best friend than my own miseries.

"I'm sorry, Jenny. I can't keep it from you any longer."

What? Was she sick like me? Did she have to be frozen? Being a scholarship student at Ridgewood, I knew she couldn't afford it. I leaned in, watching from the edge of my bed.

Angela wiped her eyes and took a deep breath. "Since you've been gone, I've missed you so much. I wanted to have something that reminded me of you." She laughed and her face brightened. "Something besides the scuff on my gym sneakers."

I scratched my head. She had plenty of my stuff. She never gave me back the books I lent her, and she still had my red sweater from the day she came to school wearing a see-thru T-shirt by accident. I gave her jewelry for her birthday, and if she could find it, I made an art project for her in sixth grade. What was she talking about?

Angela sniffed and rubbed her nose with the palm of her hand, like she always did. "I'm just going to have to tell you point-blank." She blinked. "Jenny, I'm going out with Chad."

I fell off my bed, hitting my bony butt on the floor.

Angela sighed, running her hand through her curls. They bounced back into place perfectly. "I'm sorry. We just started getting to know each other after you fell asleep. We talked all about you. He asked about you, and I told him stories…"

I got up and flicked the screen off. I wanted to eject the disc and stomp all over it, but my mom's speech was on there and hearing her talk about me made all the nasty stuff in this futuristic world go away.

Betrayal burned down my throat to my guts. How could she? She knew I'd liked Chad. Hopelessness came over me with the thought I'd been forgotten, passed up, sold out for a guy. Somehow our friendship seemed cheapened, thrown out all over a hot guy and hormones.

I hit the wall with my fist, and a sharp pain jolted up my arm. Tears rolled down my cheeks and I collapsed to the floor as guilt stabbed my heart.

Oh, Angela. Why? I missed her too much to be angry. Really, who was I kidding? I couldn't have Chad. He'd never really liked me, anyway. Was everyone supposed to put their lives on hold forever, waiting for me to wake up? It was uber-selfish of me to even think that way. Still, knowing Angela went out with Chad put a sour taste in my stomach. I had missed out on everything good and was left with high-rises, soywafers, and C-7.

CHAPTER FIFTEEN

Just One Dance

I stepped off the hoverbus, wondering why I was bothering to attend the Autumn Ball. Valex and Len had pushed me, of course, and Len even bought me a sea-green tunic with a gold-embroidered hem.

I wasn't here because of them. I needed to get out of my room and away from those videos. Ever since I learned about Angela and Chad, I just couldn't bring myself to watch any new discs. I played the old ones over and over, and that had started to rot my brain. Was this self-induced torture? I refused to admit life had gone on without me, and I was afraid of what came next. The old videos were what I remembered life to be like. They were safe.

Couples walked by, holding hands, dressed in matching tunics. I shivered in the twilight breeze, feeling so alone. Autumn used to mean long horse rides and changing leaves. Now it meant colder wind rushing on top of the high-rises and a molten color added to the smog.

I rushed into Ridgewood Prep, wanting to get the night over with. Tubes of light lit the corridors, some blinking in patterns and others solid colors, making a rainbow. The colors reflected off my skin, making me look like a mermaid underwater.

"Look at her marvel at the lights. Born before electricity, were we?"

Giggles erupted at my back, and I didn't want to turn around. I knew Exara's lush alto voice anywhere. It gave me nightmares.

Sucking my lower lip in frustration, I took a deep breath and turned. Exara shone like a giant diamond, her tunic glittering with hundreds of tiny mirrors. She'd tied her auburn hair up in a bun of twisting braids. Surrounded by her Barbie lackeys, I was outnumbered, so I just seethed in silence.

"Come on. Let's party." Exara wove her arms around her two closest friends and pushed by me. My silence worked. At least I hadn't provoked another embarrassing burn.

I stopped at the entranceway, disbelief and hope jolting through me. *Wait a second. Where's Maxim?* Weren't they going to go together?

I specifically remembered Exara and Maxim talking about their matching outfits at lunch. Maybe Maxim was already inside? I stepped into the cafeteria. Lights flashed from the floor to the ceiling and techno music blared. Apparently music hadn't evolved much in three hundred years. In this case, it had even gotten worse.

Holographic images of geometric designs were strewn everywhere, reflecting on people's foreheads, cheeks, arms and legs. I raised my arm and watched a parade of triangles stream by. Definitely an alien world.

If I'd gone to the old Ridgewood Prep Autumn Ball, the theme would have been underwater with streamers. No, I had to be here in trigonometry hell. Already my brain hurt thinking of all the equations they could form. What happened to a normal autumn theme? Like pumpkins, falling leaves, or ghosts and goblins? Had they lost touch with nature completely?

The techno music grew to a crescendo and then disappeared, silence ringing in my ears. People applauded, then all heads turned to a stage at the back of the room where Shizznizz had sat the other day, banging his head to his music in his earphones.

Maxim walked onto the stage, along with some other students. He wore a silver shirt tucked into tight, black plasticky pants. Strapped in front of him was a red guitar.

I almost fell backward. Holy crap, he was hot.

Exara stood in the front row, her multifaceted prism dress catching the light in all the right ways.

Earth to Jenny. He's already taken. By a beauty queen of a young woman, no less.

Shizznizz started banging on the drum set, and the techno beat resumed in time with his beat. The lights flashed in pulse with the music, and my heart sped in primal beats. Maxim strummed an electric chord that made my knees weak, then opened his mouth and sang.

Higher we go
To the stars
Each level we build, a new division arises
Where will you be?

In such a fragmented world
Love can be hard to find
But what is life without someone
On your level

People started dancing, but I just stared. For a second Maxim's eyes met mine across the room and his lips curved up as he sang. I blushed and looked away, disappearing behind a group of giggling girls.

Why was I so drawn to him? Was it because he was the only person at Ridgewood to pay attention to me, to talk to me like I was a person? Maybe. It went deeper than that, though, and I didn't know why. I was missing a piece of the puzzle.

I plopped down onto a chair in the back. Nothing was going to happen, so I needed to stop dreaming in the clouds. I scanned the room for someone, *anyone* to talk to. I had to get my mind off Maxim and his wonderful voice resonating deep inside my gut.

I tried to picture what Angela would do, but all I could see was her dancing with Chad in an alternate Autumn Ball three hundred years ago. I pushed all the half-empty plastic cups away and put my head on the sticky table. Closing my eyes, I wished I was at the old Autumn Ball instead, even if I had to watch Angela and Chad together.

She would never have gone out with him had I still been awake. The truth dawned on me, and I felt like the stupidest baby to ever walk the halls at Ridgewood. Angela had had a thing for Chad the whole time. She stayed away because of me. The realization hit me like a hammer in my stomach, and I blocked the party out, missing my best friend more than ever. *Oh, Angela, I'm so sorry.*

I cried until I fell asleep on the table. I didn't know how long I was out. All I remembered was hearing a disappointing shift in the music. Maxim's voice wasn't singing any longer. There was a deeper, bass voice rumbling instead. I rubbed my eyes and went back to sleep.

"Hey, Jenny, want to dance?"

I glanced up. Maxim stood in front of me. I wiped my eyes, making sure I wasn't hallucinating. There he was in all his hotness, hand extended.

I must be dreaming.

"Jenny, are you okay?"

I wiped my eyes, remembering my earlier bout of crying must have made my face all red and puffy. "I'm fine."

"Did you sleep through my whole set?"

"Yes. I mean, no." I shook my head, feeling like a complete dork.

Maxim looked disappointed, but he shrugged it off and smiled. "So, do you or not?"

"Do I what?"

"Want to dance, sillybot." It was the first time he had called me sillybot and I liked it a lot better than when Pell said it.

Glancing behind him at the flickering lights in the cafeteria, I thought about his offer. "What about Exara?"

He jabbed a finger behind him. "She's hanging out with her girlfriends."

"Won't she be annoyed?" *And, like...rip off my arm?*

"Nah. Come on. It's just one dance."

My fingers slid into his before I could stop myself, and the warmth of his skin lit my whole body on fire. He led me to the dance floor just as the fast techno song came to an end, and the bass voice began a slow love ballad. I watched the other dancers to get some kind of cue.

Maxim pulled me against him. My arms instinctively wrapped around his neck. Being this close to him was dizzying in a supremely wonderful way. Heat traveled through me until I thought that I might melt in his arms.

"Your voice is awesome." I was so impressed I couldn't stop gushing.

He rolled his eyes. "Yeah, awesome enough to put you to sleep."

I laughed and buried my head in his shoulder. He smelled like mint and spice. His chest was hard, pure muscle. I trembled in his arms, just thinking about his shirt being off. "That wasn't your fault. I haven't been getting enough sleep lately."

"Been up partying?"

More like feeling sorry for myself, watching movies of my previous life. I wasn't going to say that.

"I wish." In actuality, I'd never partied in my life.

"General Relativity getting to you?" He actually looked disappointed I hadn't called him for help.

"No. That's cool. I'm doing okay."

"Then what is it?"

"What is what?"

"What's keeping you from me?"

Um. Exara. I stared at him. Was he serious? "What's keeping me from what?"

"Being my friend."

Oh. Friend. How could such a nice word leave such a vile taste in my mouth? I was so disappointed I could have walked out that minute, but I had to recover if I was going to hide how much it hurt.

"I just can't shake the feeling I shouldn't be here. I should be dead." Stupid, stupid, stupid. Why not take him to a funeral home? Show him pictures of my dead family?

He traced my cheek with his finger. "Why would you say such an uber-sad thing? Everything happens for a reason. Maybe you just haven't found the reason why you're here."

"Back in two-thousand-twelve I wanted to save polar bears and African elephants. We all know what happened to them. My whole family's gone. Why on Earth should I still be here?"

"Maybe your purpose is staring right at you and all you have to do is open your eyes."

Boy, did I feel my mind was making things up. Was that a double meaning? He almost looked like he thought my purpose was to be with him. He was staring right at me just like he'd said.

Our eyes locked, and the world around me blurred to nothing. Even the song muted in my head. All I heard was his breath, and all I felt was his warm embrace. His head hung lower, and his lips brushed against mine.

That was it. I lost control. I stood on my tiptoes and pressed my lips against his, wrapping my fingers around the back of his neck and pulling his head toward mine. The kiss tasted sublime, taking me to heights I'd never been before. It was only after our tongues met that I realized he was kissing me back.

Fireworks exploded in my head. If anyone was to provide a reason for waking up, this was pretty darn convincing. I wanted to dance forever.

A hand gripped my right shoulder and ripped me apart from him. Exara faced me with rage in her eyes, nostrils flaring. "Stay the hell away from my man."

Her hand came up, and I had a moment of *is this really happening?* before her fist hit my jaw and I went sprawling backwards on my butt. Maxim pushed himself in front of her, trying to calm her, but all I saw was a different set of fireworks exploding into a headache.

The other students stopped dancing around us and stared. Even the music stopped. It was like the day I broke my leg. Only this was ten times worse.

Principal Hall pushed through the crowd. "What's going on here?"

A girl from my second-period class blurted out, "Exara punched Jenny."

Exara fumed, held back by Maxim. She looked like she could have punched me again if he hadn't intervened. I looked into Maxim's eyes. He looked away and shook his head. He whispered something that looked very much like an apology into Exara's ear. That hurt worse than her fist. He looked like I'd just fractured his perfect world.

The principal knelt beside me. It was the first time I'd seen him in person and not on a screen. He had more wrinkles and age spots on his face. Somehow, it made him look kinder, less fake. "Is this true?" I nodded, rubbing my jaw, which throbbed with pain.

He looked around at the other students, who all stared like I was a freak. "Witnesses?"

A few of them raised their hands. He turned to Shizznizz, who had somehow managed to slip off the stage. "Who provoked the attack?"

"She did." Shizznizz pointed to Exara. When the principal turned his head, Shizznizz gave me a wink, like he'd just done me a favor. I guess he had. I had more potential friends than I thought. I was just too wrapped up in my own problems to notice them. I glanced at Shizznizz and nodded in thanks.

Principal Hall gestured for the chaperone teachers and pointed to Exara. "Take her away. Call her parents." He turned back to me. "Come with me. I need to get a statement, file a report."

"I don't want to press charges." I was the one kissing her boyfriend, after all. In my mind, she was justified. My cheeks flamed in shame as I wobbled to my feet.

"You sure?"

"Yes. I'm fine." *Now, please go away so I can curl up in a ball and hide under a table.*

The principal squeezed my shoulder and addressed the rest of the crowd. "The next person who fights gets one week detention and probation." He put up his hands like a game-show host. "On with the celebration." The music began again, and the students started dancing like nothing had happened. Maybe nothing had happened to *them*, but my world came crashing down.

Shizznizz asked if I was all right, but I just nodded and pushed through the crowd to the bathroom. I was disgusted with myself. How could I let the dance get so out of hand? Granted, Maxim was the one who asked me to dance, but I'd practically seduced him into that kiss. I'd risen up and pulled his head toward mine, and after that, I'd stuck my tongue in his mouth.

I rubbed my hands over my reddening jaw. What would I tell Valex and Len? I'd let them down as well. The first month and I'd already gotten into a fight.

At the same time, my heart sped with exhilaration. Maxim implied I was here in this century to meet him, and then he kissed me back. He liked me. The hottest guy in school actually liked me.

A sharp pain stabbed my heart. Not enough to break up with Exara, though. The guilt was plain in his eyes. I'd put it there. His words about being here for a reason resonated with me a little too well. I almost believed him. For a moment, I felt important, part of this futuristic world. Now I felt so alienated and useless that I wanted to crawl into the toilet and flush myself down to the lower levels.

CHAPTER SIXTEEN

Rebel

"**W**hat happened to your face?" Len gently took my chin in her hands as the door closed behind me. For a second, my eyes blurred and she turned into my mom, reaching toward me through the turn of time.

"Jennifer?"

I shook my head. Boy, had Exara given me a good whack. "I'm fine. I tripped and fell, that's all." It was partially true, so I didn't feel as bad saying it.

Len came into focus, her dark eyes and long straight hair the opposite of Mom's. How could I have imagined it was her?

"You poor dear. That must have been embarrassing."

I bit my lip and nodded, not having to fake my shame. That much was true.

"C-7, get Jennifer some ice." She brought me over to the couch. "Besides that, did you have fun?"

I thought about watching Maxim sing, dancing so close, the kiss. Which answer would stir up the least amount of questions? "I guess."

"Good." She sighed in relief, like we'd both dodged a bullet. If anything wasn't happy in Len's world, I don't know what she'd do.

C-7 came back with an ice pack that had its own temperature gauge on the side and handed it to me. His eyes stared right through me. Somehow he knew that injury wasn't from a tumble on the cafeteria floor. My chest tightened and I held my breath. He tilted his head and blinked. "I hope you feel better, Jennifer."

Phew! He didn't say anything. "Thanks, C-7." I was really thanking him for his silence, and I hoped he knew it.

Len held the ice up to my chin. The cold numbed the throbbing pain. "Do you want to stay up and watch a documentary about the new recycling policies?"

That sounded tantalizing. I tried not to outwardly cringe. "No, thanks. I'm really tired. I just want to hit the sack."

"Okay." She tried to hide her disappointment by fidgeting with the ice pack, but I saw a twinge in her face.

Guilt burned in my neck and cheeks. Len was trying so hard, but she couldn't get through to me. She'd never be my mom. I took the ice pack from her hands so she didn't have to stand there holding it up to my cheek.

Len reluctantly let the pack go. "Tomorrow morning I'm making soycakes with sappy sauce."

Wasn't that every day? I nodded, wanting to make her happy. Somehow I even summoned a smile. "I'll be there."

"Great." She reached out to hug me, then brought her hand back and settled for touching my shoulder. Thank goodness. Only my real mom could properly give me a goodnight hug. "Good night, Jennifer."

I took the ice pack in my hands. "Good night, Len."

I rushed to my room and tore off my dress, throwing it under my bed to keep it from reminding me of that night. There was no way I could sleep after my first real fight. The discs called to me. It was time I stopped watching the reruns. Popping the next one in, I climbed on my bed and hugged my legs against my chest.

A Jeep rode on a trail in the bush. I got all excited. It was a *National Geographic* African safari. A whole new season I hadn't seen yet. The narrator came on the speakers. "African elephants are the largest terrestrial animal living on Earth today. Their society is grouped in family units, the head being an older female called the *matriarch.*"

Watching the majestic animals tend to their calves brought me a joy I couldn't explain. It was pure, unlike shopping for crap I didn't need or sneaking out with Angela. This feeling was way more profound, a primal need to return to my roots, even though my ancestors were from Canada and far from the African bush.

These animals had as much of a right to exist as all the humans in the world. We weren't any better or more important. This new world was animals zero (well, one if you counted Jumbo), humans fifteen billion. I had to even the odds.

Maxim said my purpose might be staring me right in the face and tonight it was. I had been confused and thought it was him, when really I was destined for much more. Sitting on my bed, I vowed to return to Martha's apartment and ask her for the information to get in touch with the Timesurfers. I was ready.

The next morning I announced over soycakes and sappy sauce, "I'm going out today."

Len dropped her spork and glanced at Valex. Obviously this issue hadn't arisen with Pell.

Pell licked her finger. "Where you gonna go?"

"Study group." I hoped that was enough information, but if they were anything like my parents, they wouldn't let me get away that easy.

Valex cleared his throat, reminding me of my dad when I asked to borrow his credit card. Even Mr. Easygoing had his limits. "Who's in this study group of yours?"

Damn! I needed a name, so I said the first name that came to mind. "Maxim."

Len looked like she'd choked on piece of a soycake. "Maxim Fairweller?"

How did they know him? Why, was he so bad? "Yeah, why?"

Len tried to hide something in her face by wiping her mouth with a cloth napkin. "Nothing. I'm just making sure it was the young man I know."

I started to get really suspicious, like a whole conspiracy was against me. "How do you know him?"

"From a parent volunteer group. He has a younger sister in Pell's class."

I was busted. They'd talk about it the next meeting for sure, and then Len would know I had no plans with Maxim. *Unless I buzzed his miniscreen.* Would he cover for me after what happened? I had no idea, but I had to find out. I'd already blurted his name across the breakfast table.

Pell chimed in, "You mean Rainy? She's my friend."

"Yes, Pell. Rainy Fairweller." Len still looked uncomfortable about me studying with Maxim.

So what? He had a younger sister Pell's age. That didn't make him an axe murderer. "So, I can still go, right?"

"Of course." Valex finished off his last soycake, chewed, and swallowed. "We want you to have friends."

Len shot him a look from across the table, but either he didn't see it or he chose to ignore it. Whatever the case, their strange behavior sparked more curiosity about the one guy I should stay away from.

Pell seemed oblivious to the strange looks her parents were shooting across the table. "Rainy breathes in a tube."

"What?" At first I thought she was joking, but the serious expression on Pell's face told me otherwise.

Len nodded. "Rainy suffers from respiratory infections. She was born immature, and her lungs weren't fully developed. Along with an inhaler, she carries a nebulizer on her back."

My heart broke. Maxim hadn't even mentioned his sister. I thought his life was perfect, but I guess he had problems as well. Were Valex and Len acting funny because of Rainy's condition? Or was it something beyond that, something tied to why hanging out with Maxim made them think twice?

After breakfast, I went back to my room and flipped the lid on my miniscreen. *Nice going, Jennifer, now you have to ask Maxim for help. Can you just say "awkward?"* I punched the numbers on the shiny card into the cybernet, but nothing happened. Had he changed his number after what happened?

It was only one kiss. It wasn't like we got married and divorced. Maybe I got the number wrong. I pressed the buttons again deliberately, making sure every single digit was correct. Still, nothing happened. I fell back on my bed and threw the card across the room. It bounced off the far wall and landed face-down on the floor. Big help he was.

From my sideways position, a slender entry point on the side of my miniscreen was visible. I hadn't noticed it before. It was the same size as Maxim's card. *Bingo.* I flung myself across the room and scooped it up. Within seconds, I inserted the shiny card into my miniscreen.

The screen showed a dot-dot-dot across it, like it was dialing, or thinking, or whatever miniscreens did. Suddenly, Maxim's face came on and I realized I hadn't even combed my hair yet.

"Jenny?" He looked like he hadn't slept all night. His usually wavy hair had a sexy curl to it, and purplish circles ringed his eyes.

"Hi, Maxim." *Calm down. Just talk business. Whatever you do, don't mention the dance, or the kiss.*

"How are you feeling? Is everything okay?"

Like I'd wallow in grief all weekend over him. I tried to keep my voice casual. "I'm doing fine. Great, really. Listen, I need a favor."

His eyes widened in surprise. "Anything. Just ask."

Yeah, go ahead, slather on the pity. It just made me feel worse. "I used your name for an alibi. Then, I learned my…guardian is friends with your mom, so she's gonna know. I need you to cover for me."

"Wow, you're quite the rebel, aren't you?"

Actually, if my real friends heard anyone say that, they'd laugh their butts off. "Um. Yeah. Right. Anyway, we're supposed to be studying this afternoon at the school library, okay?"

He nodded. "Got it. Studying at the library. No problem."

"Great." I breathed with relief. "Thanks. Thanks a lot."

"Sure. Any time." His eyes sparked with hope and I wondered just what he hoped for.

Don't think too much into it. End the conversation. Now. "See ya." I moved to press the eject button, but his voice stopped me.

"Listen, Jenny?"

My finger hovered over the key. "What?"

He ran his hands over his face. "I wanted to talk to you about—"

"Don't worry about it, okay? I'm over it." My voice had an unusual edge to it. I sounded like my mom when she was on the phone with a telemarketer.

"You're over it?" Hurt weakened his voice.

"Yeah. That was *so* last Friday. Come on."

He seemed disappointed, but I wasn't about to give him therapy. He'd have to talk to Exara for that. "Gotta go. See you in homeroom."

I ejected the card before he could respond. Sure, I felt a bit mean, but I didn't want to talk about how he thought of me as a friend all day. Yeah, a friend with benefits. Trying not to feel too bitter, I pocketed his card and packed a bag for Martha's high-rise. This time I took my old pocketknife for self-defense.

I jumped on the hoverbus to Martha's apartment. I felt guilty lying to Valex and Len, but visiting Martha was something I had to do. I didn't think they'd understand. Besides, if the Timesurfers were as secret as Martha said they were, I didn't want to involve my substitute family. No reason for them to get in trouble on my account.

When I got off the hoverbus, the platform was empty. No sign of the green-haired gang. I remembered the way, blocking my nose against the smell of old carpet and oil. If this place was considered an upper level, I couldn't imagine what the lower levels looked like. *Probably something like a third-world country.*

Martha answered on the first beep and let me in. "Look who got into a fight."

"It was nothing." I looked away, unable to lie to her too. "Just a mean girl at school."

Thankfully, she let the subject drop. "I didn't think you'd come back." She looked so happy to see me, I felt guilty asking her for more information. I didn't want her to feel used. I really was glad to visit her.

"I'd love to spend more time with you. How's Jumbo?"

"He's sleeping." She nudged him with her toe and he purred softly. "Sleeps a lot nowadays."

I couldn't imagine investing all of my money in a pet and then having the pet age before my eyes. "I brought you something." I held out one of the precious discs from my collection. "It's a *National*

Geographic episode about African lions. I know it's not housecats, but it's the closest thing to it."

"Oh, Jennifer, how kind." She took the disc and held it up against her frilly yellow apron by her heart. "I think I have an adapter somewhere around here. I'll watch it tonight."

"I thought Jumbo would like it."

"He'll be jealous, but he'll live." She walked into the kitchen and my stomach knotted up dreading her tea. "Black, green, or cranberry?"

Oh, more options this time. "I'll try cranberry."

As Martha puttered around in her kitchen, I bent over and reached toward Jumbo. *Just one pet.* I wanted to feel animal fur under my fingertips, hoping it would bring me back to my previous life. A miniature furry time machine.

Jumbo cringed back, hissed and showed his teeth. I bolted back up. *Guess not.* Rejected by the hottest boy in school *and* the only cat left in the world. My weekend sucked.

Martha came back in with two china cups of steaming tea. At least my tea smelled better this time. I took a sip, allowing the bitter taste to rest on my tongue so it didn't choke me. Martha sat next to me, swirling her dirty water with her silver spoon. "So, did you think about it?"

"About what?"

"The Timesurfers."

Wow, this was going to be easier that I thought. "Actually, I did."

"Good. A girl your age needs to make decisions about her life."

"I want to meet them. How can I get in contact?"

"Here." She stuck her hand into a pocket in her apron and pulled out a small black card, the same size as the one Maxim had given me. "Code word is web of life. It's an older code, but it should still work."

"What do I say?"

"Tell them your history and you're interested in their programs." She sipped her tea. "You can say I sent you."

I took the card in my hands and rubbed my finger over the imprinted number. "Wow. Thank you, Martha."

"You bet. Anything to help a fellow cryosleeper."

I pretended to sip my tea. "You never did tell me why you were frozen."

Martha raised her eyebrows. "Motorcycle accident."

"A motorcycle hit your car?"

"No, I was on one. No helmet, of course. I was pretty wild back in the day."

I tried to picture sweet little old Martha on a motorcycle, and my imagination didn't stretch that far. "What happened?"

"I was speeding. I was late to my boyfriend's birthday party. We were all going to surprise him, and I had the cake tied to the back of my bike." She smiled. "Ryan Summers. He was a keeper, all right. Blue eyes, blond hair, and smelled like the woods after a rain."

I thought of Chad, then Maxim, then forced my brain to stop thinking. "Sounds handsome."

She laughed to herself. "He was. If it wasn't for the roads being slick and that damn squirrel." She shook her head. "Doesn't matter now, does it?"

I could see it mattered to her. "I'm sorry I brought it up."

"Nah. It's good to talk about it sometimes." She put a hand on her neck, rubbing her skin. "The motorcycle flipped and I was thrown off. I remember flying through the air like a bird. Time stopped. You'd be surprised how many things I thought of in that instant—worry for the cake, love for my parents, my life with Ryan. It all flew through my mind before the ground came up. I broke my neck in the fall. I could see just fine, the wet road, the overturned cake, white frosting melting into the grass, but I couldn't feel anything. My entire body went numb.

"The doctors said I could live my life as a quadriplegic or freeze until some new scientific development on regenerating stem cells was made. Ryan said he couldn't live seeing me like that. He eventually got a scholarship to study law and stopped visiting." She waved her hand. "I don't blame him. His whole life was ahead of him, and my life was at an end. Or so I thought. My parents paid for the cryosleep procedure, and the rest is history."

The tea churned in my empty stomach like acid. I frowned and shook my head. "That's horrible."

She patted my hand. "That's life."

Martha's story summoned courage inside me. If she could go through so much, I could get over Angela dating Chad. I could put away the sadness of missing my parents and Timmy. I wasn't about to live my life in a small apartment with a cat. I needed to go out and do something to change this screwed-up futuristic world. "I'm going to call them. I'm going to see what I can do."

Looking years older than she had a few minutes ago, Martha placed her empty teacup on the arm of the couch. Jumbo jumped into her lap and purred. She smoothed over his fur with her crumpled, knobby hands. "Good. It took me too long to figure out that time only goes forward. It doesn't go back. You can either catch up with it or let the loss swallow you whole."

CHAPTER SEVENTEEN

Real

When I got home, I couldn't wait for dinner to end so I could insert that black card in my miniscreen. Pell decided to brief us on her entire day, including how she tricked C-7 into washing the already-washed dishes. Valex and Len marveled at her cleverness, and I blended into the background, slurping up my muddy-brown soybean stew.

I even swirled my finger around the bowl to make it look like I'd enjoyed it. "Can I be excused? I still have a lot of homework to do."

"You've been doing homework all day." Len gave me a suspicious look and I remembered I was supposed to have been studying with Maxim. *Not the best excuse.*

"Let her be. She's trying to catch up." Valex winked. How much did he know?

Len pursed her lips. "Don't work all day, dear. You need to have fun sometimes, too." Her words jolted me, and my spork clanged on my plate. They were the same words I would throw at my real mom when she turned me down for a shopping trip or dinner out. Guilt trickled through me. Here was a nice, new mom trying to spend time with me, and I was throwing it all away.

I couldn't change the feelings in my heart. I didn't want Len, I wanted my real mom. The truth made me hate myself for taking their time, invading their lives. I folded my napkin and summoned a polite smile. "Thank you for a wonderful dinner."

"Thanks for eating with us, Jenny." Pell spoke with her mouth full. She looked so cute in twin braids sticking out on either side, I almost wanted to stay and play Pixie Swap with her.

"You're welcome. Bus ride tomorrow?"

She gave me a thumbs-up. "You bet!"

I walked slowly to my room, but when I closed the door, I ran to my miniscreen and whipped out the black card. The familiar dot dot dot came on the screen and I waited, hoping Martha's connections weren't outdated.

The screen flashed and a man with spiky blue hair and three glittery nose rings stared back at me. His eyes traveled the entirety of my bruised cheek before meeting my gaze. "Yes?"

"Web of life." Even as I said it, I felt stupid, like I was in some type of James Bond movie.

The man narrowed his eyes. "Who gave you this number?"

Was I going to get Martha in trouble? I hoped not. "Martha." Hoping the first name would do, I waited as a knot tightened in my chest.

"One second." The screen went blank and I wondered if he'd severed the connection. It was like I was walking on Christmas ornaments and egg shells, waiting for something to crack. What kind of people was I dealing with?

The man came back on the screen. "What do you want with us?"

I cleared my throat and tried to project my most authoritative voice so I didn't sound like some kid. "I want to learn more about you."

"This isn't a school project."

"And I'm no normal schoolgirl."

His eyes narrowed, and I realized he wasn't that much older than me. "What's so special about you?"

I crossed my arms. "Only the fact that I'm three hundred and twenty years old."

His face softened and he seemed to see me for the first time. "You're a cryosleeper?"

"The richest one in all of New England. Now, are you going to tell me where to find you or do I have to hunt you down?"

He cracked his knuckles, finally looking interested. "Our next meeting is this Friday night. I'm sending the coordinates to your miniscreen. High-rise thirty-two seventeen G, level twenty-four."

Geez, that seems pretty low. Is it a lower level than where Martha lives? I certainly hope not.

"Come alone. No recording allowed. Code word paradise."

"Got—"

He ended the connection and the screen went black.

I shook all over, cold sweat dripping from my chin.

Could I do this?

I had until Friday to figure it out.

School seemed trivial compared to the larger issues in my life. I couldn't concentrate in General Relativity, and I sat by myself at lunch, a good seven tables from Maxim and Exara. Whenever Maxim looked in my direction, I pretended to be interested in my soybean mush.

The afternoon was a big boring mishmash of uneventful classes. When the techno jingle finally rang, I shot up, yanked my miniscreen's wire from my screendesk, and bolted out the front doors. I stepped onto the hoverbus in relief, glad the drama of Ridgewood Prep was over for yet another day. I shuffled to the back and plopped down in the last seat, putting my head back and closing my eyes.

"Anyone sitting here?"

I looked up in disbelief. Maxim held onto the center pole, steadying himself as the hoverbus detached from the ramp. It was too late. I had nowhere else to go. "No."

"*No* as in no one's sitting here, or *no* I can't sit here?"

I crossed my arms and gave him a nasty look. "Both."

"Great." He turned away, then turned back toward me again. "I really need to talk to you."

I was about to tell him to go to hell when I realized he was my alibi, and I'd need another one if I was going to attend that meeting on Friday. "Okay, but my stop is in twenty minutes."

"Twenty minutes isn't a lot of time."

What did he want to talk about? The last three hundred years? "That's what we've got."

"Okay." He sat next to me, his leg warming the side of mine. The seat wasn't *that* small. He could have spread out, leaned against the window, or kept his thigh to himself.

"I'm sorry about your jaw."

The entire left side of my face was purple as a plum. I would have gotten a lot of raised eyebrows, except everybody had already heard about the embarrassing fight. "It's nothing."

He touched my chin, bringing my face up toward his. I felt his breath on my cheek. "This is not nothing."

I was tired of dancing around the point. Now was as good a time to ask as any. "Why the hell did you ask me to dance?"

Maxim dropped my chin and looked away. "That's what I need to talk to you about."

The hoverbus reached the first stop and a rush of people walked on and off. Maxim waited until the bus started up again. *Five agonizing stops left.*

"Exara's family and my family have a kind of understanding, an agreement of sorts." He ran his hand through his silky black hair. "My family lives in her father's high-rise."

"She owns the whole building?"

"Her father does, yes."

"Wow."

"Wow is right. Anyway, my parents got into financial trouble a few years ago, losing billions of people's credits in investments, backing a recycling factory that refused to process living matter for fertilizer."

"What's living matter?"

Maxim sighed. There were dark circles under his eyes. They were bigger purple-black rings that could give my jaw a run for its money.

"It's people, Jenny. They recycle everything else around here, so it was only a matter of time before they got around to people. There's no place to bury the dead, and it's cheaper than conventionally fertilized food for the people in the lower levels. The government has to do something to keep them fed or they'll revolt."

"Oh, gosh." My stomach hollowed and a squirmy feeling crawled over my shoulders.

"My family believes in what's right, and we stuck to our choices even when the factory went out of business and was bought out. My father's had a tough time finding a job since. With my sister's lung condition, living in the smog and mildew choking the lower levels is out of the question. So, extreme measures had to be taken to ensure Rainy could live in a place where she wouldn't get sick."

Maxim trailed his finger up and down the silver pole. "Exara's father lets us stay in the apartment for free because she and I are going out. It worked fine until I got to know her and realized I didn't like her anymore. If I break up with her, my whole family may have to move to the lower levels. I'd have to quit Ridgewood and go to work in the factories, and Rainy would get sick."

He looked into my eyes. "I'm not saying it wasn't worth it, but kissing you put all that on the line."

The thought of a little girl getting sick and dying because of me made me nauseous. The whole situation seemed like something out of a screwed-up soap opera that had run for too many seasons. "You really think Exara's dad would throw you and your family out if you two broke up?"

He leaned back in his seat. "You know Exara. What do you think?"

"That's *so* not fair. It's not fair to her, either. You can't pretend to like someone."

"It worked out fine for a while. I mean, she's a beautiful girl. Anyone would be excited to go out with her. Everything was fine until I met you."

I backed up against my side of the seat, like touching him would turn him to stone. This world I'd woken up in was so cold, so cruel. How could life get this bad? "I don't want to get involved. I don't want your family thrown out on my account."

"I knew that was what you'd say. That's why I debated telling you. I don't want to push you away. I want you to know the kiss we shared was real."

I blinked as his words sunk in. Then my heart tore. He liked me. He actually liked me more than Exara. Unfortunately, we could never be together. Not with so much on the line. The hoverbus stopped again, and this time Maxim got up.

"Wait!" I grabbed his arm.

He looked at me hopefully, as if I'd figured out some way to trick the universe. If I had, I wouldn't be on the hoverbus—I'd be back in 2012.

"I need you to cover for me again this Friday night."

He looked away, shaking his head, and I wondered how disappointed he was. "I can't keep doing this. You're going to get caught."

"One more time. That's all I ask."

Everyone had filed off the bus, and he only had a few seconds before he missed the stop. I felt so bad keeping him there, but I needed him. If he truly liked me, he'd help me out. Maxim signaled to the hoverbus driver to buy us more time.

"Okay. One more time. Where do you go, anyway?"

The hoverbus driver got up out of his seat and shouted down the length of the bus. "Do you want to get off or not?"

"Go!" I waved my hand. "I'll tell you later."

Maxim nodded. "Bye, Jenny." He ran down the length of the bus and jumped off without looking back. The doors closed and the bus detached from the ramp. I told myself I wouldn't look out the window, but I did anyway. Maxim stood on the platform like a homeless person, staring at me in the seat we had shared, as the hoverbus took off.

Too bad for him I didn't specify when "later" would be.

CHAPTER EIGHTEEN

Paradise

The longer I rode the hoverbus to high-rise 3217 G, the sketchier the people became. Some of them had clothes resembling ripped T-shirts and jeans from my generation. I sat next to one woman with more holes than jeans. Were her clothes from my generation? Maybe the new styles just didn't permeate the lower class.

My outfit began to stick out, the exact opposite of what I'd wanted. At the bottom of my pile of hand-me-down clothes, there was a black tunic with a hood and matching black boots that came up to my knees. Len said clothes like those were only worn on formal or solemn occasions, like funerals. So, I had snuck out of the apartment and wore it to the meeting. I wanted to look like I was serious about this, not some rich high-school playgirl doing it for a thrill. But now, all it did was scream *rob this rich girl*.

We traveled farther from the center of the city and closer to this massive cement wall that reminded me of the Great Wall of China. I had no idea what the wall did, because more high-rises were beyond it. Did buildings cover every square inch of the world?

When my stop came, I pulled the hood around my head and signaled the driver. It wasn't a preprogrammed stop on the route. Hopefully he'd honor my request.

The hoverbus stopped, and I stepped onto the platform.

The driver cast me a questioning stare before he left, like I'd gotten off by mistake. I waved him off, pretending to know what I was doing by digging in my backpack. The hoverbus sped away, and

I felt abandoned even though I'd chosen this for myself. What was I doing here? Why couldn't I just accept my new life?

Because I'd be living a lie. I'd be ignoring my dreams, and I'd end up just like Martha, an old lady with a replicated cat. Cracking my knuckles, I entered the building.

The temperature in the hall seemed colder than outside. There were no lights, so I opened my miniscreen and used the white background of a new document to light my way. I had two or three hours of battery left. Hopefully, I wouldn't need the light for that long. The air had a wet, mildewy smell, like old dish towels left in the sink for too long. I wrapped my arms around myself and looked for an elevator. Old soybean wafer wrappers, broken glass, and tattered plastic bags lined the hallway. I kicked my way through. How could anyone live like this?

Did anyone live here? I listened for voices, but the walls were as silent as a graveyard. That made me think about conveyor belts carrying bodies into recycling plants, and I shivered and cursed myself for thinking such scary thoughts in such a creepy place.

I reached an elevator and slapped the panel, but nothing happened. The buttons were all blank. Great. I'd have to take the stairs all the way down to level twenty-four. Checking the time, I only had twenty minutes. This didn't seem like the type of thing you could wander in late to.

I found the emergency stairs and booked it, leaping two steps at a time. Debris on the stairs slowed me down, but I kicked it away and kept going, making excellent time. I watched the painted numbers descend from seventy-three down to forty-two.

Only twenty more to go.

Working up a sweat, I jumped onto the next landing, right in the middle of something squishy.

"Hey! Watch where you're going,"

I scrambled back, covering my mouth with my hand to prevent a scream. My miniscreen bounced on the floor, illuminating the old woman's face in fluorescent light from her hairy chin up. She crawled out from under a pile of sleeping bags, a woven ring of plastic bags on her wispy-haired head.

"I'm sorry, ma'am." I wanted to keep going, but she blocked the way. *Should I mention the meeting? Does she need a code word, too?* By the look of her tattered clothes and toothless mouth, I didn't think so.

She gave me a suspicious glare. "What are you doing down here?"

"I...I'm going to meet someone."

She snorted. "Not here you ain't. This building is condemned."

I felt like the walls would fall in around me, crushing me to death on the spot. "Condemned? How?"

"Mold infestation. They kicked everyone out. Said I couldn't live here no more. This place is all I got, you see." She paced back and forth, swinging her finger through the air, making me nervous. "I'm not gonna start over, work my way up from level one all over again."

"I'm sorry."

"Sorry ain't gonna cut it." She shot me a nasty pout, her whole bottom jaw extending way past where it should. "I hid here in the stairwell. I was doing fine until you came along."

"I won't tell anyone." I put up my hands to show my innocence. "I'm just passing by."

Meanwhile, seconds ticked by on my miniscreen. I had to get going. I dug in my pockets and brought out a soywafer. She looked like she hadn't eaten in days. "Here, you take this. I have a bunch at home."

The old woman snatched it up, tore it open, and shoved the end in her mouth. I bent down slowly and retrieved my miniscreen. "If anyone asks, I didn't see anyone up here. I swear."

I slowly stepped around her as she sucked on the soywafer. With no teeth, it would take her a while to eat the whole bar. Enough time for me to get away. "You just keep going on living up here, okay?"

She didn't answer, so I shuffled down the next flight. I listened over my shoulder, but no footsteps sounded, so I increased my pace, practically jumping each flight at once.

Ten more levels to go.

My whole body shook from the strange encounter, and my knees weakened until I worried they'd give out. *Come on, Jenny; you've made it this far. You're sure as hell not going back up there.*

What if no one was on level twenty-four? My skin crawled with the thought of climbing all the way down here to an abandoned room.

No. Martha would never send me to these people if they weren't for real.

How well did I really know the old woman, anyway? I'd only met her twice, but it was a bond that had to be trusted. She'd gone through everything I had times ten. If Martha said to contact these Timesurfers, then they were here.

By the time I'd convinced myself to keep going, I reached level twenty-four. I pushed in the door and a waft of dusty air came out. Slipping inside, I glanced down the corridor. A shadowy figure of a man stood at the end. My heart beat a thousand times in that one minute.

"Are you alone?" His voice sounded grizzly, like he'd smoked cigarettes his whole life.

Besides the old crazy homeless woman? I cleared my throat and my voice quivered. "Yes."

"Good." He stepped forward and I took a step back, ready to make a run for it. At that point I didn't care if I ran into ten homeless crazies on the way back up.

"Code word?"

I paused. That wasn't something an axe murderer would ask. Then I remembered my conversation with the blue-haired man. "Paradise." My voice croaked.

He opened a door and waved his hand inside. "Welcome to the Timesurfers."

CHAPTER NINETEEN

Just Like Me

People of all ages, social classes, shapes, and sizes filled the room, some standing, some sitting on the dusty floor. A wallscreen, lit by an energy cell hung at the room's center, showed an unknown galaxy of stars. I recognized the blue-haired man across the room. He nodded as I came in, his nose rings glinting in the light from the wallscreen. I took a seat on the floor in the first row, next to two young women dressed in upper-level tunics like mine.

I breathed in clean air and noticed an air purifier connected to their battery cell in the center of the room. If they took that much care of their people, then they couldn't be that bad, right?

The guard stuck his head inside and nodded to the blue-haired man. "That's it, Jax. They're all here."

Had they been waiting for me? My cheeks flamed, and I leaned over until my hair fell on either side of my face. I practiced my art of blending into the wall. How good I was at it, I had no idea, but teachers never called on me in "wall mode."

"Excellent." Jax stood at the room's center in front of the wallscreen. He wore a black jumpsuit over his lean body, reminding me of a ninja. An animal-rights ninja. *Pretty darn cool.*

"My name is Jax Upton. I'm the president of the Timesurfers, and I welcome you to our recruiting meeting tonight." His eyes skimmed the crowd, remaining on mine for a little longer than the rest.

He extended what looked like a lipstick container into a long, silver baton and pointed to the screen. "This is the Aquarius Dwarf galaxy, the home of a newly found Earthlike planet orbiting in its sun's habitable zone."

I squinted my eyes, but all I saw was a cluster of shiny stars.

The tip of his baton tapped one of the glowing spots. "Paradise 15. It's roughly earth-size with an orbital period of two hundred and ninety days, a little shorter than ours. This planet is twelve percent closer than we are to its sun, but the star is dimmer, lower in temperature, and smaller than our sun. This means the greenhouse warming is similar to Earth's. Surface temperature would be seventy-two degrees Fahrenheit."

Audible gasps rang out around me. The young woman next to me jumped up. "When was it found?"

Jax crossed his arms and met her gaze. "Our scientists found it two days ago. Which gives us some time." He addressed the rest of the room. "Due to the recently established planetary laws, the first to walk on the planet claims it. This means we'll need a mission set in place—a ship and a team of cryosleepers—by the end of this year."

"Do you think you can beat the government to it?" An older man with a white beard spoke as he typed wildly into his miniscreen.

"We have to. Out of all of the planets we've scanned, this one seems the most promising for our mammal regrowth program. It's too far away for the government to consider mining operations— only for colonizing. We're going to need people who can withstand the cryosleep process without difficulty. We can't take the chance that our team won't wake up once the ship reaches Paradise 15."

I whispered to the young woman beside me, "What do they mean, without difficulty?"

She tucked a piece of her brown hair behind her ear. "Forty-seven percent of cryosleepers don't wake up."

I swallowed hard. Wish I'd known that before. But what was I complaining about? I'd woken up. I was alive. Back in 2012, they hadn't had the research statistics yet. I must have been the other fifty-three percent.

"We'll conduct initial screening tests for all applicants shortly. I must warn you—anyone who goes is taking a chance. This planet may not be inhabitable, and you'll be forced right back into cryosleep. Either way, it's a sacrifice. When you return to Earth, everyone you know will be gone. Our descendants will continue the program, and they'll be here to greet you. If the planet is habitable, you will begin the DNA replication to create a world in which people can live in harmony with animals and nature. The point is not to colonize the planet with a bunch of people, but to have a small team who will act as guardians for the animals until they can live on their own."

I raised my hand.

Jax turned to me and nodded.

I took a deep breath, surprised I was even speaking. He'd gotten my attention. I wanted to know more. "How many scout ships have already gone out?"

"We've sent fourteen teams of cryosleepers into space, one for each Paradise planet found. Since they're all hundreds of years away, the results are upcoming."

No proof. My stomach sank to the floor. Why was I always involved in the experimental projects?

The older man in back spoke before I could ask more questions about the process. "Why not let the government tackle this themselves?"

Jax's eyes grew hard, like two ice lakes. "Because they'd mine the resources from each planet just like they did on Earth and, soon, the moon. The human race would spread through the universe like a virus, killing everything in its path." He clicked his baton and the silver end retracted back into the handle. "The cycle of unsustainability stops here on Earth."

The older man had stopped typing. "How can you be sure the government will honor these planetary claims?"

Jax didn't skip a beat. "The World Coalition has put them in place. Our nation can't afford to start another war. The other world governments are way behind on space travel technology, so if we set foot on this planet and set up home, we'll be able to control the colonization efforts."

The older man slapped his miniscreen down. "Sounds like a shot in the dark, if you ask me."

Jax shrugged. "Then you don't have to join us." His gaze traveled through the rest of the room. "I'm taking applications for volunteers. Those of you who'd like to work in our DNA preservation facility, talk to Ralk here on the right. Those of you willing to donate to our cause, talk to Yara by the door. Those of you with nothing to lose, brave enough to scour the galaxy, see me. All I need is one drop of blood."

People bolted from their seats and the room turned into chaos. I stood like a lost child wondering where its mother had gone. Sure, I wanted to donate and, according to Len, I had the funds to do so. The real reason I was here was to make sure animals lived once again. To be with them and study them.

My dad's words came back to me. *When you wake up, you'll be cured. You'll be free.* Living in this skyscraper hell was not the freedom he imagined for me. He would have wanted me to follow my dreams.

Before I could convince myself otherwise, my feet took me to Jax. Where my courage came from, I had no idea. Maybe I was just fed up with this futuristic world.

No one else stood in his line.

Jax looked me up and down. I searched his boyish face to see what he saw in me, but he gave nothing away. He reminded me of some futuristic Peter Pan. "You wish to apply for the team?"

I shrugged. "Everyone I know is already dead and gone. I have nothing to lose." Besides, what were the odds I'd get chosen for such an honorable task? Surely they had people already in their organization battling it out for a ticket off Earth. If I was chosen, I'd deal with it then. I could always change my mind. At least I could rest easy knowing I'd tried.

He took a plastic strip from his miniscreen. "What was it? Three hundred years?"

I nodded. "Long enough to see the world go to hell."

"You think you can fix it all by yourself, just because you knew what it was like to live in the good old days?"

I nodded, angry at everything—my cancer, Chad, Maxim, the tick of time. I jutted out my chin. "As a matter of fact, I do."

His lips broke into a sly smile. "You're just like me."

Looking at his ninja bodysuit and muscles, I hardly thought so, but I wasn't about to argue. Jax touched the plastic strip to my finger, and I received a small zap of electricity. When he pulled the plastic away, a drop of blood the size of a pinhead blossomed on my fingertip.

He checked the plastic. "That's it."

An explosion rattled the floor underneath me, and the lights flickered. A guard burst into the room as everyone stood in confused silence. "We've been compromised."

Jax shouted over my head, "Everyone, get out." He stuck the plastic strip into his miniscreen and jammed it in a backpack. Meanwhile, others disassembled the equipment. They unplugged the wires from the energy cell and the lights went out. Someone screamed, sending shivers up my spine.

This is so not happening.

It really was. People scrambled out the front and back doors as another explosion shook the walls. Jax ordered his guards to leave with the equipment. Big burly men scooped up the energy cell and scurried out the back door.

I turned to follow when there was a crash behind me. The wallscreen had fallen on top of Jax as he ejected the memory disc. I had to get out of there, but Jax had my blood, and I didn't want whoever was knocking on the door to come to Valex and Len's looking for me.

I ran to Jax and tried to lift the screen. The small muscles in my arms bulged as I strained, gritting my teeth and growling in frustration. "It won't budge."

"Here." He gave me the disc. "Get it out of here."

I held the shiny circle in my hand, the most incriminating piece of evidence there was, and I had no idea how to get away. "No. You're coming with me. I'm not going to leave you."

I looked around in desperation. We were the only two people left in the room. *Man, these Timesurfers sure know how to shuffle.*

He winced in pain. "You have to get away. You and the disc are too important."

Men shouted and laser fire sounded on the levels above. *Dammit!* I scanned the room for anything to prop the wallscreen up with. Nothing.

I put my hands under the wallscreen. "Help me lift it. On the count of three."

"One." The laser fire grew louder until it sounded like they were in the corridor outside.

"Two." My blood pumped so fast through my veins that my neck twitched with each beat.

"Three."

We both heaved, and the wallscreen rose just a bit. It was enough for Jax to pull himself out. I helped him up and gave him back the disc. "How do we get out of here?"

Jax stuck the disc into his pocket and hobbled over to the window. "It's the only way."

"Are you crazy?"

He threw a chair through the glass and the window shattered. Cold, windy air rushed in, chilling my arms. Pulling a metal device out of his backpack, Jax strapped the bag over his shoulders. "Come on."

Men burst through the door armed with lasers. They pointed in our direction. "Freeze."

Jax grabbed me and jumped out the window.

I screamed like I when was on the Expedition Everest, although this time there'd be no picture taken of my shrieking face.

As we fell, Jax fired a grappling hook. At first I thought he had missed, but something yanked us up in the air and toward the building. He braced our collision with his legs, and there we stood. On the side of the building. At least ten floors up.

"Don't look down." Jax held me against him.

If he let go, I'd fall to my death. I wrapped my arms around his neck and shrieked.

"I'm not going to drop you." He hooked the end of the rope to his belt and walked along the side of the wall. "Can you reach the next balcony?"

"I'll try." My voice squeaked out. Above us, the men with the lasers hung their heads out the window where we'd just dropped. They fired down at us, trying to shoot around the balconies, and Jax increased his pace. The balcony came up quickly and I reached out, my fingers slipping on the metal. We swung like a pendulum to the other side.

Jax reached out and grabbed the fencing around a terrace. Lasers shot around me, one of them singeing my hair. I felt my ear just to make sure it was still there.

"Hold on." Jax threw me over the railing and I landed on firm, solid ground. Wilted plants surrounded me, their soil dried and their leaves falling off. A single sour tomato dangled in front of my nose. Jax climbed in after me and disconnected the hook. I thought the ordeal was over, but he pulled me up. "Come on. It won't take them long to figure out which window we went in."

I scrambled up, dizzy and sick, and followed him into an apartment filled with trash. A putrid scent wafted up from the floor and I covered my mouth with my sleeve. Jax pulled out a flashlight. Pillaged garbage stood in heaps. A plastic couch had been gutted, the cushions ripped to pieces. Old food waste grew mold along the arms. At least that's what I thought it was. Strange objects, like old dolls and pots and pans, dangled from frayed wires along the walls.

Jax pulled me forward toward the front door. We spilled out into the hallway, gagging. Now I knew why they had condemned the building. Climbing over heaps of trash and old clothes, we managed to locate a stairway. Jax yanked the door open and we slipped in. He took a few steps down.

"Aren't you going the wrong way?"

"They're swarming the building. The only way to escape is to go farther down."

My stomach pitched. The farther down I went, the worse it got.

"We don't have much time."

I had nowhere else to go. I had to trust him. Taking a deep breath, I followed Jax down the stairs. The darkness was absolute, and the cold worked its way under my clothes to prickle my skin. Jax's small flashlight was the only beacon of hope in an endless rush of trash, muck, and stench. How could people live in such filth? I was disgusted and horrified at the same time. In the years I'd been asleep, poverty had increased while the select few lived in the upper levels with the dwindling resources Earth had left. I couldn't imagine what the third-world countries had been reduced to. Probably unlivable desert. Suddenly, Jax's mission to Paradise 15 didn't seem so farfetched.

We reached a door, covered in rust, that looked like it hadn't been opened in ages. Jax threw away an old mattress propped against the handle. "This is it. Level one."

Before I could protest, he kicked the door open and we ran into an alley between buildings. Twilight hung over the city. Had I missed curfew? If Valex and Len called Maxim's apartment, I was so dead.

The alley between the buildings was so narrow that I could spread my arms across it and touch both walls. Hovercrafts crisscrossed in the sky overhead. So many people in the upper levels lived in denial of the filth they lived on top of. It was mind-numbing.

"This way." Jax led me down three blocks and into a larger alleyway, big enough for cars, if they had still existed. He brought out his miniscreen as sirens wailed behind us.

"What are you doing?"

"Calling for help."

Men shouted down the alley from which we'd come.

Anxiety bubbled in my veins. I bounced up and down on my toes and grabbed at his arm. "They're gaining on us. We have to move."

"Just wait."

What? Did he have some type of cloaking device? If so, why hadn't he used it back in the room, before we went flying through the air?

The men's footsteps grew louder and I backed away from the corner, ready to make a run for it without Jax if I had to. The wind roared above my head as a hovercraft lowered from the sky. Cans skittered in the whirlwind and my hair whipped around my face as the craft hovered over us. A hatch opened from the side and the guard from the meeting lowered a rope. Jax grabbed on and gestured for me to join him.

Some men rounded the corner and started firing at the hover-craft. I ran and grabbed onto the rope. Jax grabbed the rope with one hand and slid the other around my waist. The hovercraft rose in the sky as someone pulled us up. Below me, the men grew smaller until

arms grabbed onto me and pulled me inside. My heart beat franti-
cally as the roaring wind turned into deafening silence. Panting, I
rolled on my back and closed my eyes.

"Geezum hell, are your meetings always like this?"

CHAPTER TWENTY

Resemblance

"**N**o. Our meetings are usually much more prosaic." Jax laughed with a crazy edge to it as he recovered beside me.

"Here, Jennifer."

I opened my eyes. The guard from the meeting offered me a bottle of water. I accepted, gulping. My throat was parched. "Who were those people?"

Jax sat up against the hull and took a swig of water. "Mercenaries. Hired by rich people in the high-rises to steal our information."

"What do they want to do with it?"

"They want the planets for their descendants."

I wiped the water from my chin. "Why can't everyone just live on Earth?"

"You've seen it. This planet won't last much longer. When the end comes, it's gonna be bad. Everyone wants to secure a future." Jax capped his water bottle and stuck it in his pocket. Who knew ninja suits could hold so much?

"With so many people after you, how did you know to trust me?"

He rolled up his sleeves. There was a tattoo of a rose and a name scrawled in loopy letters: *Sophie*. Who was Sophie? It wasn't a futuristic name. "Martha's been our informant for many years." Jax's eyebrows twitched. "She would have made a good scout, except she decided too late and didn't pass the cryo tests."

"So she told me."

Jax leapt up like we'd just had a picnic in the park and he was about to fetch the dog. "We have to get you home before your parents worry."

"They're not my parents."

"I know." Jax gave me a steady look as if to say he understood my pain, all in one glance. "Where do you live?"

I closed my eyes and recited the letters and numbers, glad I'd taken the time to memorize them.

"Good. Stay here. You'll be home in no time."

Jax walked to the front of the ship, and I sat by myself, wondering what the hell had just happened and what I'd gotten myself into. I'd met real people who shared my dream. At what risk? Part of me wanted to hole up in my room and watch those old videos for the rest of my life, and a more rebellious, adventurous part of me wanted onto that scout ship.

The hovercraft slowed and the hatch opened on the platform where the hoverbus usually dropped me off. Jax snuck back and offered me a hand, helping me off the ship. "I hope all this didn't scare you away."

I looked into his face, wondering how old he really was. Nineteen? Twenty? Old enough to be my older brother but not old enough to be my father. What was his story? Why did he risk so much?

"Nah. When you've been frozen, everything else is like a dream." He took his hand back and stepped into the hovercraft. "Or like a nightmare."

He was so right, but I ignored it. Now wasn't the time to whine. "Are you going to contact me about the next meeting?"

His eyes lit with surprise, as if he didn't think I had what it took. "It will take us a while to recover from tonight, but yes, I'll be in contact."

"Thanks." I turned and started walking.

"Jennifer."

I whirled around. "Yeah?"

"Thank you for saving my life."

Me? The hero? More like he saved mine times ten.

Before I could respond, the hatch closed and the hovercraft drifted away. I walked back into the apartment feeling like I'd just been thrown into an episode of CSI.

The next day, I awoke to my miniscreen beeping like an oven with the timer going off. I rolled over and slapped the enter button, thinking it was some type of alarm. Maxim's face flashed on. "Jenny? Are you okay?"

Damn! Why didn't it tell me it was an incoming call? I shot up in bed. "Maxim? What time is it?"

"It's ten. What? Did you party all night long?"

More like I ran for my life all night long, but if I told him that he'd never cover for me again. "No, I had trouble sleeping."

"I wanted to check on you to make sure you were okay."

I ran my hand through my hair and stuck chunks of tangles behind my ears, not even wanting to know how messy it must have looked.

"I'm fine. How are you?" *Really? Is that all you can come up with?*

Maxim rested his chin on his hand. He hadn't shaved. A line of stubble added to his allure. He looked so hot that I had to look away and think about soyloaf to cool down.

"When are you going to tell me where you're going?"

A knock came at my door and Len's voice drifted in, "Jennifer, the last stack of soycakes is going cold."

Saved by soycakes. Who would have thought?

"Coming, Len." I shouted over my shoulder, then turned back to Maxim and shrugged. "You heard her, I can't talk right now. I have to go."

"Is it a guy?" His voice dripped with jealousy.

I thought of Jax and his blue hair, nose rings and upturned mushroom nose. *Totally not my type.* "No. Definitely not." Maxim had no right to be jealous. It wasn't like I was his.

Maxim sighed. "All right. I'll stop pestering you. I'm just glad to see you're okay. I was worried about you all night."

My cheeks warmed and I pulled my hair out from behind my ears to hide it. Maxim thinking about me all night made my body hot all over. Then Exara came to mind and his apartment with his entire family hanging on the line. Guilt eclipsed my hormones.

"Don't worry about me, okay? I can take care of myself." My words came out a little harsh and I wished I could take them back, but I had to push him away.

"Sure." He blinked, looking away as if I'd slapped him. Emotion flooded his face and he swallowed it down. "Bye, Jenny."

The screen went blank and my heart sank like the Titanic. Why did I feel so jilted? He cared about me, even called me, and yet the whole conversation felt empty. Like a promise he couldn't keep.

Another knock on my door startled me out of my sad haze. "Jennifer, are you coming?" Pell kicked the door impatiently with her little foot.

"No. I'm not hungry." I slumped on my bed. "Tell your mom to put them in the fridge. I'll eat later."

"Mom!" Pell scampered down the hallway toward the kitchen.

Sure, I felt guilty bailing on them for breakfast, but after the conversation with Maxim, I couldn't bring myself to get out of bed.

Like the last few nights, I turned to my videos to take away the pain. Popping the next one in, I waited for the screen to flash on and curled up on my bed.

Angela laughed and waved at the camera. She wore a graduation robe in the deep navy-blue of Ridgewood Prep, with a gold cord tied to her cap for being on the honor roll. "Hi, Jenny! I can't believe so much time has passed and I haven't made a video for you." She stuck out her lower lip. "I feel so guilty. I haven't forgotten about you. Not at all."

Angela turned the camera toward a newly planted tree in the rows leading up to Ridgewood. "The senior class got together, raised some money, and planted this in your memory."

Great. A tree. That helps me so much. I rolled my eyes. Where was this tree now? Buried by skyscrapers? Still, the thought of everyone getting together to plant it in my honor gave me chills.

At the base of the tree, she focused the camera on a golden plaque. *Jenny Streetwater 1995-.* The other date was left blank.

Usually a memorial had two dates, which made it seem so unre-solved. I wondered how long the tree stood and how many students passed by it saying my name.

Angela held up her left hand, the leaves rustling above her fingers. "Every time I walk by it, I think of you."

The diamond on her left hand glittered in the sunlight. *No. It can't be.* I leaned over to get a better look, but Angela brought the camera back to her face. "There's something else I have to tell you." She bit her lip and gazed up at the sky, smiling at a delicious secret. "Something big."

I sat up on the edge of my bed, hugging my miniscreen in my lap. There were no comforting stuffed teddy bears to hug in the future.

She flashed the ring. A princess cut with two sapphires on each side. "Chad asked me to marry him. I know it's so soon after grad-uation, and we have college coming up. We're both going to USM. After we graduate...well, you know what."

I bolted up on my feet and pressed pause. Angela's smiling face stared back at me, frozen in time. It wasn't her perfect white teeth that caught my attention. I traced a lock of her curly dark hair. The same color as... My chest tightened. I needed to find C-7.

Running from my room in my PJs, I bumped into Len.

"So, you're up for those soycakes after all?"

"Um...sure." I could have agreed to eat soycakes for every meal for the rest of my life. Anything to get her out of the way. I pushed by her and into the kitchen where C-7 loaded the dishwasher.

"Good morning, Jennifer. I trust you slept well."

"I need you to do a search for me."

C-7 scanned the living room, and I wrapped my hands around his arm. The metal felt cold and hard under my fingers. I whispered, "Please. There's something I need to know."

He checked the hallway, but Len had gone back to her room. Valex and Pell sat on the couch playing Pixie Swap. His head buzzed as he glanced down at my hands on his arm. "Very well. Give me your search parameters."

I nodded, trying to find the courage to say what I suspected. "I need to know who Maxim Fairweller's ancestors are, from my gener-ation in two-thousand-twelve. Is it anyone from Ridgewood Prep?"

C-7 blinked, and his head buzzed like a computer during a really big download. "Affirmative."

My heart jumped to my throat and thought I was going to be sick. "Who?"

"There are several strands of the family tree, but one leads directly to two students attending the same years as you."

It was too much of a coincidence to be made up. I knew the names before he said them.

C-7 stared at me, and although his eyes should have been cold, a spark of compassion glowed there. "Chad Foster and Angela Buffet."

I fell back against the wall fridge and slumped to the floor.

"Jennifer, are you okay?"

"No." I'd kissed a descendant of the boy I used to like and my best friend. Combined. How screwed up was that?

C-7 put a cold hand on my forehead. "Your temperature is two degrees above normal. Should I call for Valex and Len?"

"No, no, no." They'd ask me what I was upset about, and I couldn't talk to anyone about this. It was just plain too weird. "I'm fine. I just need to go back to my room and rest."

As I stumbled away, gripping the wall for support, I realized why I felt such a connection to Maxim. He had everything I liked about Angela inside him, along with Chad's hotness. The thought of kissing him made me excited and squirmy at the same time. Was it like kissing my best friend?

My head ached just thinking about it. I pulled the disc adapter out of my wallscreen and sank back into bed, cursing myself for watching another window to the past.

Those videos were like a game of roulette. Every other one shot me in the foot. Or more like the heart.

CHAPTER TWENTY-ONE

Eighteen

Two weeks later, I sat on my bed, checking my miniscreen for any messages from Jax or Maxim. Nothing. Nada. Zip. Zilch.

I tried the Timesurfers for the zillionth time and no one answered.

Maxim's card rested on my dresser, gathering dust. He sat with Exara every day at lunch, stealing guilty looks at me from across the cafeteria. I tried not to look in their direction, but every so often I couldn't help it, trying to find a part of Angela's face inside his. It took me a while to get over the grossed-out factor of my mixed-up relationships, but after I accepted it I found myself drawn to Maxim more, as if spending time with him would recapture what I had had with Angela. He was a gorgeous guy and a best friend combined. But I couldn't have him. Even if he liked me back. Just thinking about it tore me apart, like reading *Romeo and Juliet*. Except we weren't dead.

In an effort to focus on the present and not the past, I stayed away from the videos and spent time with Valex, Len, and Pell. Pretty soon, a whole month had passed since I'd seen any of my real family's faces. At first, I was scared I'd forget what they looked like, that their features would blur in my memory. That didn't happen. I could still picture Mom's bright eyes and the stern, quizzical face Dad made whenever Timmy threw one of his toys. Things were as normal as they could be living three hundred years in the future with a substitute family and no animals besides a cloned cat who hated me. My life sounded like a sitcom that was destined to fail.

"Want to help me pick a birthday present for Pell?" Len stood in my doorway, jolting me out of my miserable reverie.

I had homework to do, but I needed to get away from my miniscreen and out of my room before my head burst from boredom and waiting for things that would never happen. "Sure."

"Excellent. Valex took Pell on a sightseeing trip to the greenhouses, so we can use the wallscreen in the living room."

I stood up, gave my miniscreen one last backward glance, and followed Len into the hallway. *What if it beeps while I'm gone?* I had to face reality—if no one had called me for weeks, no one was going to call me in the twenty minutes it would take to choose a present for Pell. I had to detach myself before I started plugging the battery cord into my arm.

"I'm so thankful for all the time you spend with Pell." Len settled onto the couch and turned on the wallscreen.

"She's a sweetie. I love her."

"She looks up to you. She's always wanted a bigger sister." Len didn't move to search the cybernet.

What's on her mind?

She never did anything random. Every move seemed like a gentle nudge. My heart quickened. Did she know about Maxim or the Timesurfers?

"When we heard you'd be awakened, I was nervous to bring someone into our house. Yes, Pell wanted a bigger sister, but I didn't want to disappoint her if you didn't like us and wanted to live somewhere else."

"Besides my real home in 2012, I'd never want to live somewhere else. You and Valex have been so welcoming. If I'm quiet, it's my fault. Getting a new family and having everyone I know being gone is hard."

Len put a tentative hand over mine. Her fingers were dry and cold. "I can't imagine. I'm always here if you want to talk."

"Thanks." For a second, I considered telling her everything—my feelings for Maxim, going to the Timesurfer meeting, missing my family. But I couldn't bring myself to say any of it out loud. The hurt cut too deep for words, and speaking of it would only magnify the pain.

"I wanted to let you know you've exceeded all of our expectations. You're a brave young woman, and I know you'll do wonderful things in this world."

Guilt came over me like sappy sauce, all sticky and sickly sweet. What would she say if she knew I'd applied for a scout position with the Timesurfers, leaving them all behind? I kept my mouth shut. I wasn't sure I'd go through with it anyway, even if they picked me. The thought of entering cryosleep again still freaked me out.

"So, what are you thinking of getting Pell?"

Len pressed a panel in the arm of the couch and the search engine for the cybernet flashed on, a glimmering pixel leading to infinity. She typed in Pixie Swap, and a dozen options filled the screen, from pink, fuzzy pixie slippers to pixie tunics and higher-leveled games.

"Wow, she'd like everything up there." I pointed to the slippers, noticing how the sides glittered like fairy feathers. "I really think she'd like these the most."

"That's what I thought." Len pressed a button and added the slippers to her virtual shopping cart.

"Your birthday's coming up, soon, too. The big eighteen."

More like three hundred and two plus eighteen, but I didn't correct her. "Yeah, it's hard to imagine I'll be legal to make all my own decisions, to vote." Although, in this day and age, I had no idea who to vote for.

"Have you thought about what you want?"

I slumped back against the couch. No one could give me what I really wanted—a hug from my parents, a ride on Thunderbolt, a game of Transformers with Timmy. Funny how life worked. When I was with them, I wanted a salt-water fish tank, an African safari, material things. "No."

"Valex and I talked about throwing a party for you, having some friends over."

I pictured Exara coming over loaded with insults and Maxim meeting Jax. My brain short-circuited. "That's not necessary. Really." I had to think of something quick before she sent out invitations. "How about we celebrate as a family, just the four of us?"

Len smiled.

Thank God. The last thing I wanted was my complicated life put on display.

"That would be wonderful. What a great idea."

"I'd love to watch some movies from my childhood. I know Pell would like some of the cartoons."

Len nodded. "I can arrange that. Give me a list and I'll see what's still downloadable."

"Okay. I'll work on it."

"Thanks for helping me."

"No problem." It was actually kinda fun. The exchange with Len broke a barrier in my heart. I was growing to like her gentle way of persuasion. Even though she wasn't my real mom, she was pretty cool. "Anytime."

Len shifted uneasily on the sofa. "I'm not expecting you to ever call me *Mom.*" She picked at a hole in the couch with her fingernail. Sadness tinged her normally bright eyes. "I know what it's like to lose someone you really care about. How the loss eats a hole out of your soul until you think you'll never feel complete again."

I stared in silence. I'd never seen a crack in Len's composure. I didn't think such a thing like crying happened in her perfect world.

Len breathed deeply. "I know I put up a good front. It's my defense. My mom died in a hovercraft accident when I was Pell's age. Since then, nothing's ever been the same. Putting a smile on helps me convince myself that life goes on."

"I'm sorry. I didn't know—" I was such an idiot to think Len had never felt my pain.

Her bottom lip quivered. "My aunt stepped in. So did my grandmother and my older cousin. None of them could replace her, even if they wanted to."

All this time I'd thought she was trying to take Mom's place. I'd built a wall of resentment against the one person who could truly understand me.

Len straightened, dabbing at the corner of her eyes. "I should have told you sooner."

"No." I wiggled closer, putting am arm around her shoulders. "I'm glad you told me now."

Something beeped from the hallway, and we both jerked up and laughed. I still wasn't used to all the new noises in their house. "Is that the dry cycle on the dishwasher?"

"No." Len listened, titling her head. "Sounds like your miniscreen."

My miniscreen! I raised my eyebrows in an unspoken question.

"Go." Len smiled.

I bolted to my room, falling over my feet twice on the way. By the time I reached the door, the miniscreen lay silent. The side blinked with a promising yellow light. Whoever it was must have left a message.

I closed the door to my room for privacy. My hands shook as I flipped up the lid. Jax's boyish face flashed on, nose rings glittering in crescent moons. He still wore his ninja suit, the collar standing up around his neck. His blue hair stuck up at all angles in spikes like some manga character.

"I'm sorry it's taken me so long to get back in touch with you, Jennifer." He leaned forward. "It took us a while to recuperate after the last meeting. The good news is the organization has reviewed your files, verifying the information you gave me at the meeting, and you're invited to join our ranks. A tour has been scheduled for all of the new recruits next Saturday at noon. Be at your hoverbus platform on time, and a hovercraft will pick you up and bring you to our secret underground facility."

His face grew serious. "Of course, if you've changed your mind, that's completely acceptable as well. Simply send a message to this new miniscreen's address and let us know." His eyebrows rose and his blue eyes glinted, shining like the color of his hair. The hint of a smile touched his lips, like he already knew I'd be there and he was only mentioning the last part out of formality. "I look forward to serving in the Timesurfers with you."

The message flickered out and I stood there gawking. *The Time-surfers want me?* Was it because of my previous experience with cryosleep, or the fact I was alive when animals were around? Or the fact that I'd saved their leader from sudden death?

Whatever the case, I had to act fast. I needed an alibi for Saturday, and Maxim had already said he was done helping me out. I tried to think of anyone else, but I hadn't really made any other friends at

Ridgewood Prep. At least not any that I could trust with something so epic.

No. I needed to talk to Maxim, tell him the truth. It wouldn't be easy, but if I knew him as well as I thought, he'd understand that the Timesurfers fulfilled my life's dreams and wouldn't get in the way. It was a gamble, but asking Maxim was the only chance I had.

CHAPTER TWENTY-TWO

Dreams

"**W**hy do we have to take the early hoverbus?" Pell twirled her braid around her finger. She still had two soycakes on her plate, and we needed to book it to the platform in the next three minutes.

I checked the wallscreen. Seven twenty-two. *Make that two minutes.* "Because there's something important I need to do."

"What?"

How could I explain the complicated mechanics of my, Maxim's, and Exara's relationship to a seven-year-old? "I need to talk to someone before class. Listen, you don't have to go with me. I'll take the early bus, and you can catch the next one."

"But we always sit together."

"Geez, Pell, it's only one morning. What did you do before I woke up?"

She sniffed. "I sat alone. All the time."

Major guilt trip. Had Timmy sat alone on the bus? I blocked the mental image of him holding a plastic Transformers lunchbox all by himself. *Earth to Jenny, you're in twenty-three-fourteen.*

Her little pout almost changed my mind. "I've gotta go. If you want to sit together, you have to come with me now."

"Fine." Pell stuffed the last two soycakes in her mouth and grabbed her lunch container. Her cheeks puffed out like a squirrel's mouth full of nuts. She chewed all the way to the hoverbus. Thank goodness there were a lot of people waiting in line to board, or else it would have taken off by the time we got to the platform. Guess this earlier bus got more action.

We found a seat together in the back. "You all right?"

She swallowed and rolled her tongue around her mouth. "Uh-huh."

"Good."

Pell kicked her feet against the seat. Thump thump. Thump thump. What would happen to her if I joined the Timesurfers and scouted the universe for Paradise 15? If she missed me for one morning, she'd miss me all her life, just like Timmy. I tried not to think about it too much.

"Your birthday's coming up." I tickled her and she giggled, crumpling forward. "I know what you're getting!"

She clapped her hands together. "What?"

I shook my head and smiled. "I can't tell you."

"Pretty please with sappy sauce on top?"

"Nope." I zipped my finger across my mouth. "My lips are sealed."

"Then I'm not telling you what you're gonna get."

I straightened up. "What?" Since when did a seven-year-old know more than me?

"You heard me."

Now she has attitude? I sat back, contemplating a bargain, but her stop came up and she jumped out of her seat and gave me a kiss on my cheek, like she did every day. "Bye, Jenny."

For some strange reason I got all teary-eyed. "See ya, Pell."

Her little black braids bounced as she ran to the door. Maybe it was better I didn't know what Valex and Len had gotten for me. I'd just feel guilty anyway. I didn't need any presents for my birthday, especially from my substitute family. They'd already done so much for me, and I could barely make time to spend with them.

I didn't have time to think about my birthday any further, because Ridgewood Prep came up in a gleaming façade of glass, and I pushed toward the front of the bus. When the door opened, I practically leapt off the hoverbus and ran to homeroom. If I was lucky enough, Maxim would get there before Exara and I'd have a few minutes to set up a time to talk.

That's if he wants to risk everything to talk to me. Again.

Swallowing doubt, I settled behind my screendesk and tapped my fingers impatiently. Sure, I could try to send him a message with the screendesk, but I hadn't mastered all the intricacies of the privacy settings. I didn't know if everyone could see it, or if the principal could read every correspondence that went through. I wouldn't put it past them and I didn't want to chance it. Besides, it was hard to get the tone of the message right. I didn't want to leave a video message on his miniscreen. Too much evidence. It would be much better to talk to him in person.

Students shuffled in, and I tried not to stare at the doorway. Exara strutted in between the screendesks wearing pink high-heeled boots and a minitunic, and my stomach sank. I'd wished it was one of her "beauty treatment" days, but I wasn't so lucky. In fact, she hadn't missed a day since the dance. She gave me an evil sneer and settled into the seat in front of me. Was her perfect attendance a ploy to keep Maxim and me apart?

Maxim ran in two seconds before the techno jingle, and I crashed my head down on my desk. The one morning I decide to come early, he was late. Maybe it just wasn't meant to be.

As I brainstormed another way to get an alibi, a miracle happened. Principal Hall came on the main screen with the announcements, and Exara left her seat, asking to use the bathroom. Maybe an eyelash was out of place.

Seconds after she turned the corner, I whirled around. Maxim was sleeping on his desk, the fluorescent light illuminating the side of his face like a ghost.

"Psst."

He didn't budge, so I shook his arm. "Maxim, wake up."

"W-what?" He glanced up through waves of dark, luscious hair, hair I wanted to run my fingers through.

"I need to talk to you."

"Oh, okay." He straightened in his seat, a curious spark in his eyes. "What about?"

I couldn't explain the Timesurfers in the two minutes it would take for Exara to redo her makeup and come back to class. Besides, I needed a more private place to talk. "It's a long story. Can we meet up sometime?"

Maxim looked down, drumming his fingers, possibly calculating the risk. "I'll be at the fencing club after school."

Fencing? That sounded kinda scary. I had a hard enough time with volleyball. "Do I have to join?"

"Nah, just say you're coming to try it out."

I weighed my options, which were close to nil. "Okay."

"I'll make sure you're my partner and then we can talk."

"While we're fencing?"

"It's the best way to ensure privacy."

He was right. Seconds ticked away with me blatantly leaning across his screendesk. One fist to the jaw was enough. "Sure." I whirled around and turned on my screendesk. By the time Exara came back, I was typing furiously about theoretical physics, creating a theoretical distraction.

"Trying to cram?" She flashed me a wicked grin.

I ignored her. *Yeah, I could cram it all the way up your...*

Cue the techno jingle. This time it came at the perfect moment, before I could open my bitter mouth. Everyone bolted up, like they sat on hot potatoes, or I guess it would be soytaters nowadays. I still hadn't seen a whole vegetable or fruit in all of our overly processed meals. Maxim passed by my desk, giving me a slight wink before his wave of hair fell in front of his face.

Mission accomplished. Appointment made. So why did my stomach gurgle in protest? Now I had to tell him the truth. I hadn't confided in anyone in over three hundred years. Well, maybe Martha, but it was easier to talk to someone who understood my situation.

The rest of the day moved at a turtle's pace, if turtles still existed, of course. I kept rehearsing what I was going to say over and over. I had to admit I was excited to have a meeting planned with him, even if it was during a sport I had no prayer at. I reminded myself this was strictly business. Maxim needed me as much as he needed a thorn in his side.

The fencing team met in the cafeteria, so as the last bell rang, I headed straight over. Shizznizz met me at the door, his hair, more red than orange today, stuck up in a Mohawk. "Hey, Jennifer. I didn't know you were into fencing."

"Oh, I'm just trying it out." My voice sounded so lame I was surprised he didn't see right through me. He gave me something from a box by the door; it looked like part of a broom handle. "Great. Here ya go."

"This isn't a sword."

He grinned. "Press the side button."

I did, and the handle zinged in my hands. Purple light shot out in the form of a medieval sword, thick and heavy like King Arthur's Excalibur. I almost fell backward on my butt in surprise. "It's a laser sword!"

"Yeah. What did you expect, some tiny silver thing?"

"Isn't this dangerous?"

I shrieked as he waved his hand through the light stream, thinking he'd never play drums again. His fingers slid through the light unharmed. "It only reacts to other swords. Something about the frequency..."

I swung the light sword in an arc, pretending I was in a video game. "You don't have to get all technical." Fencing wasn't the real reason I was there. Although, after swinging that light sword, I reconsidered.

I don't have time to join a fencing team. Not when the Timesurfers are knocking at my door.

"Watch this." Shizznizz put his arms around me and pressed another button on the side. The sword changed into a samurai katana blade. He pressed it again, and I held a black dagger. The handle's weight changed with each weapon, making it feel like I held real steel in my hands. "You can select the type of weapon here."

"This is amazing."

He still had his arms around me. His voice grew deeper. "So, you have a partner?"

"She's already taken." Maxim spoke before I could respond.

Shizznizz's arms flew up, and I whirled around. Maxim wore a white jumpsuit with the front half unzipped just enough to tease me with a glimpse of a totally ripped chest, hard as a statue by Michelangelo. I tried not to stare and failed miserably. "So you play music *and* fence?"

"I'm loading my resume with activities so I can apply for a decent job when I graduate." Maxim offered his arm.

I slid my hand underneath like I'd done it a thousand times before. "You think laser sword fencing is going to make an impression?"

He shrugged, leading us to a quiet part of the cafeteria. "Maybe. You never know what qualities companies are looking for."

We walked to the same spot where we'd kissed that night at the Autumn Ball. I wondered if he'd chosen the spot for a reason, but he didn't seem to notice.

"What do you want to do when you graduate?"

Maxim turned on his laser sword, and it glowed into a golden Spartan warrior blade. "I want to be on one of the first teams that mine minerals on the moon."

I chose the medieval sword, thinking the size would protect me even though it weighed down my wrists. "Why?"

"I'd make a ton of money. I'd be able to support my family within two years." He lunged and our swords clashed, the light buzzing as they touched.

"That's a long commute."

"You're telling me. They're saying average shift will be six months on, one month off."

The fact that Maxim would give up so much to take care of his family impressed me. He was like a knight in shining armor, and he had the sword to match it, too.

"Think about your defense. Try to predict my next move."

Maxim lunged and I fell back swinging. I didn't even know the footwork. But, I wasn't here for sword fighting, I wanted to talk without Exara suspecting anything. So, I had to make it look like I knew something about fencing. My sword met his as I regained my footing. I pushed back against his weight, and we met in the middle, our faces a centimeter apart as our swords clanged.

His eyes soaked me in and I steadied my shaking knees. "You're stronger than you look."

The cryosleep must have done something to me, because I had never been this good at anything gym-related. Or Maxim was letting me win. "There are a lot of things you don't know about me."

He leaned in farther, and his lips almost brushed mine. He arched an eyebrow playfully. "Don't I?"

Now was the time to tell him. I breathed the spicy scent of his after shave. "I had dreams, like you do."

His grip softened, and our bodies pressed together, interfering with the light of the swords. "Where are they now?"

"They're still there, only they've changed. They had to because of what's happened to the world."

His face grew serious, complicated. "Is this what you wanted to talk to me about?"

I nodded, glancing at the fading glow of our swords. "You said at the dance my purpose may be staring me right in the face. Well, I found it."

"You did?" His voice was so shaky, I glanced back up. An eager expectation lit his eyes.

My voice fell to a light whisper. "Have you heard of the Timesurfers?"

The muscles in Maxim's chin tightened. His face was guarded. "I've heard of them."

"You know how I always wanted to help animals? These people want to bring them back." I swallowed and held his gaze steady to attempt to look like he couldn't change my mind. "They've invited me to join them."

Maxim pulled away, shaking his head. His sword fell to his side and flickered out. "Cyberhell, Jenny. Joining the Timesurfers isn't like joining the fencing team."

"I know." After Jax's and my runaway escapade, I knew what I was getting into. I couldn't tell him about the danger or he'd never let me go.

"They're not well-liked. Some people call them crazy fanatics with suicidal plans."

I thought about Jax and how he'd saved me and then thanked me for saving *him*. "They're not crazy. They only mean to do good."

"Yes, but sometimes doing good gets you in a tough place. Believe me, I know about choices."

I remembered how his dad had lost the company when they decided against recycling more than artificial plastics. Yes, he knew about sacrificing for ideals.

"Well, this is my choice. Are you going to help me or not?"

He put up his hands like he was helpless. "What do you want me to do?"

"I need you to cover for me on Saturday. They're giving a tour of the facilities, and I want to be there."

Maxim came up and grabbed my arm, pulling me against him. "Is this really what you want? Can nothing else make you happy?"

I nodded; the magnetism drew me into his velvety lips.

"Nothing else?"

My heart ached to close the distance. If I said I wanted nothing else, I'd be lying. "There are some things I can't have."

His forehead touched mine and he leaned into me. "Me, too."

The world could have ended right then and I wouldn't have known. I could only stare into the flecks in his eyes and feel him against me, caressing the flame that shivered in my chest.

"Since when did fencing require romance?"

We both turned, breaking the spell. Shizznizz stood next to us with a purple katana.

Maxim growled, "If you don't mind."

He shrugged. "Just looking out for ya, man. Wouldn't want word to spread about a new form of duel."

I ignored Shizznizz's implications and stared at Maxim. "Saturday?"

Maxim rubbed a hand over his face. "Yeah. You're all set. Go."

I clicked off my sword. Our cover was blown anyway. My fencing time was done. "You'll figure something out?"

Maxim walked toward the door as if he couldn't handle being near me.

I died a little inside.

"I always do."

CHAPTER TWENTY-THREE

Candidate

I avoided Maxim for the rest of the week. Whenever we were together it was like some ancient volcano that was close to erupting, and if it exploded, it would take Ridgewood and everyone in the school along with it. Besides, I didn't want him to have the chance to tell me he'd changed his mind.

On Friday night, as I sat in bed and contemplated my complicated life, my miniscreen beeped with a message from Maxim. *Saturday, school library, twelve PM study group, b there or b square.* I smiled, thinking about how Maxim always came through for me, even when he didn't agree with my choices. My alibi was set. All I had to do was walk to the hoverbus platform at noon.

I had no chance of sleeping a wink. Instead, I popped in the next video in my collection. A younger-looking Valex came on the screen, scruff peppering the hard lines of his jaw. Had Valex mixed this video up with one of his from his youth?

"Hi, Jenny." A deep voice with a subtle confidence rang alarm bells in my ear. I hiccuped with surprise. It was Timmy. All grown up. His curly hair had grown in front of his eyes, and he shoved it back in a practiced gesture.

"I know I haven't talked to you in a while, but I wanted to let you know I think about you all the time. Every day, I walk by that tree at Ridgewood with your name engraved in gold and wonder when you'll wake up. When I was little, I hoped you'd wake up when I was your age and we could, you know, like, hang out. I'm your age now, and you're still sleeping..." Timmy's eyes clouded over.

I shivered with sadness. I couldn't be there for him when he needed me the most. I missed his prom, his graduation, his college years. Everything.

Someone in the background yelled his name and Timmy waved. "I'll be right there."

When he looked back, his eyes were clear. "Anyhow, graduation is in a week. I'll be going to NYU and then on to law school."

Law school? He'd blindsided me with a truck. What happened to the Transformers? I thought he wanted to be an astronaut. I blinked and Timmy had aged fifteen years. My hands shook as I dug through the discs in case I had missed one, but this was the next one in the pile, number twenty-seven out of thirty-one. Thirty-one. My heart sank to a place where I couldn't find it. I only had a few more left. It was like holding on to a safety line and then finding out the threads were cut at the end.

Why didn't my parents have themselves frozen when they got sick? Or Timmy? Why make me the only one of us to have a second chance? My dad had enough money to freeze the whole family.

A coldness gripped my chest, and I broke out in goose bumps. Something must have happened suddenly, something with no physical way for any of them to be brought back.

I slammed my hand on the wallscreen and the video flicked out. I decided I'd rather stay in blissful ignorance. My reasoning was flawed. Keeping the last few videos unwatched was somehow keeping them alive. If I didn't know how they ended up, I wouldn't have to come to terms with the fact they all had died at some point. It was like happily ever after movies that ended when the couple got married. Ended on a good note.

Scooping up the rest of the discs, I looked for a place to hide them from myself. Someplace where I wouldn't be tempted. I didn't have the heart to destroy them. Someday I might find the courage to know the answers to my past. Steeling my nerves, I climbed on my bed and stuck the pile on top of the recycling chute, shoving them all the way back, out of reach. With nothing else to do, I collapsed on my bed, tossing and turning for the rest of the night. Timmy's fuzzy cheeks and hard-edged face kept coming back to me, but I refused to accept the new Timmy. I wanted to remember him the way I'd last seen him, as a toddler with Elmo in his hands.

Morning came with a renewed hope. If I was looking to the future, then I wasn't mired in the past. The seconds ticked away to noon, and I pulled a black tunic sweater with a high-collared turtle-neck over my head. I zipped up my thigh-hugging boots. I didn't have a ninja suit like Jax, but this ensemble was close enough. With three-inch heels, I could take on the world.

Valex, Len, and Pell sat on the couch distracted by some sort of documentary on recycling, so it wasn't hard to say good-bye. I jogged to the hoverbus platform and checked my miniscreen. Eleven forty-five.

I felt like an overeager dork arriving so early, but I knew in this case it was better to be early than fashionably late. Three hoverbuses came and left as I waited, each driver staring at me like I was crazy not to get on. I wondered if they were paid by the hour or by the passenger. Geez. I could have been waiting for someone to arrive.

I kicked the edge of the platform. How would I know which one was the transport? Would Jax be on it? I wanted to see him again. There were so many questions lingering in my mind, one involving a certain someone named Sophie.

A black hovercraft that looked more like a giant wasp than a means of transportation slowed and pulled up to the platform. The hatch opened and no one came out.

My heart thumped in my chest. Was this it?

A woman with short black hair and a pointy nose, wearing a white lab coat, stepped onto the platform. I recognized her from the meeting. Yara. The woman Jax had said to talk to about donations.

Yara strutted toward me, turning her face so her nose pricked the air. "Jennifer Streetwater." I nodded and she extended her hand. "Yara Heifmesiter."

Her fingers were long and cold, and I felt the opposite of welcome as I scrounged up some polite words. "Nice to meet you."

She sniffed the air and dropped my hand as if it smelled foul. "Follow me."

Yara whirled around on her heel, leaving me to follow. This was it, the moment of no return. If I wanted to go back, I had to act now. Every molecule in my body wanted to be on that ship more than anything. I was tired of the universe telling me where to go. It was about time I made my own decisions, shaped my own destiny.

I jogged to catch up to her, my boots clomping on the ramp. Without looking back, I ducked through the hatch. The interior was much nicer than the hoverbuses, or even Valex and Len's hovercraft. A heated rush of air caressed my face. Seats with plastic cushions lined the walls and the center aisle, much like on an airplane. Two people sat in the back. Light techno music drifted around me. I took a seat next to the window and belted myself in.

Yara sat across from me in the aisle. She popped open her miniscreen and her spidery fingers flew over the keys. I looked to the back. A young girl with orange pigtails and freckles kicked the seat, her shiny silver tunic scrunched up around her calves. A woman with gray hair tied in a bun and a plain tunic that reminded me of a brown paper bag sat beside her. I smiled, but they ignored me. Feeling stupid, I gazed out the window as the hatch closed and the hovercraft sped away. The buildings passed in an endless tide.

Yara flicked her eyes up from the screen. "Jax tells me you're a cryosleeper."

I nodded, surprised. So many people danced around the subject, and she brought it up like asking if I enjoyed ice cream.

"He said you were...especially brave." Her eyes were like darts. I shrugged and cowered back against my seat, looking away.

As Yara read further down her screen, she furrowed her thin eyebrows skeptically. "You were asleep for over three hundred years?"

"I was." I looked her straight in the eye, for once proud of the fact I could be her great-great-grandmother.

She raised an eyebrow. "Any side effects?"

"Side effects?"

"You know—loss of memory, dizziness, shortened life expectancy."

My eyes widened. "I certainly hope not."

"Well, the doctors would have told you by now." She scanned me from the tips of my boots to the wisps of hair around my ears. "You look fine. I'll put that down as a no."

I remembered the drop of blood. "You're the ones who took my blood. What are the results?"

She flicked her fingers over the screen. Her eyes darted back and forth as she read. "Looks like you're one of the lucky ones."

I thought of Martha. Was she a lucky one? She certainly wouldn't think so.

Yara tapped a few keys, narrowing her eyes. "So, you excel at science and biology."

I thought back to my junior-year grades, minus gym. Mom had pressed me to take AP biology, and I had had a crush on the teacher, so I paid more attention than usual. Besides, I got to do a project on equestrianism. "I guess so."

"And you've had experience working with real animals?"

"I volunteered at a veterinary clinic. I spayed and neutered animals, and even set a broken leg on a Doberman." I was especially proud to see that dog walk again. That was one of the moments in my life that I realized I was meant to help animals.

Yara raised one eyebrow and continued to type. As she read more about me, the corners of her mouth tightened into a bitter frown. She pushed her screen down and it clicked into the keypad. "You're a great candidate."

"For what?"

"For the team, of course." She shifted as if her seat had grown cold. Was that competition shining in her eyes? Could someone already established in the organization possibly be jealous?

Before I could tell her I was still thinking about whether or not I wanted to go, the hovercraft dropped and my stomach flipped. I gripped the seat rails with sweaty fingers. Outside, the levels flew by as we plunged to the alley floor.

"What's going on? We're going to crash!"

"Nonsense." Yara leaned back in her seat. "The trap doors slide open at the very last moment."

Trap doors?

The ground came up quickly, and I squeezed my eyes shut, expecting every bone in my body to shatter on impact. Instead, we glided down, past the trash in the alley. Dark walls came up on either side as the hovercraft tunneled down into the earth. I wrapped my arms around my shoulders as a claustrophobic heaviness weighed on my chest. What if the driver moved sideways one inch and the wingtip hit the side of the shaft?

I looked over my shoulder at the girl and woman in the back, but they didn't seem fazed by the super-secret entrance. The girl slept on the older woman's shoulder. Yara's eyes were closed, her lips set in a small smile, like she looked forward to returning home. I tried to settle down, pushing the rising current of dread back down my throat.

Bright light flashed up from below, and the ship lowered us into an underground loading bay the size of a small village. Hovercrafts like the one we were on were parked in neat rows beside us. People in white lab coats scurried beyond them in a glass corridor that ran along the perimeter. On the side, a row of guards in dark ninja uniforms, much like Jax's, held lasers at their sides at attention.

Excitement tickled the hairs on the back of my neck.

Yara spread her hands. "Welcome to the official headquarters of the Timesurfers."

CHAPTER TWENTY-FOUR

Sophie

The hatch opened slowly, like the gateway to another world. I followed Yara down the ramp with the girl and the woman behind me. The air felt cool and stale with no trace of wind. How secure was this facility? Would we be scrambling around in another raid?

The panels in the ceiling above us whirred as they came together, sealing the entrance. The chrome plates hit with a boom, reverberating in the pit of my stomach. We could have traveled to the center of the Earth for all I knew. *Yeah, no raid today.*

A man stood at the bottom of the ramp. Although his back was turned, I'd know that thick swirl of blue hair anywhere. A wave of calm came over me. After what we'd been through, I was safe in Jax's presence.

Yara rushed down and threw her arms around his neck. For someone so uptight, she sure knew how to chuck herself at a man.

Jax gave her a quick squeeze and turned to me. "Jennifer, I'm so glad you decided to join us today."

I stopped before stepping off the ramp. "I can't wait to take this tour."

His lips widened into a grin that rivaled the Cheshire Cat. "Fantastic."

Yara turned toward me with a cold stare. "Wait here with the others while I get the tour host."

"That won't be necessary." Jax stepped toward me. "I have a break in my schedule, and I'd like to take these wonderful people around."

Yara's mouth clamped shut. As the leader of the Timesurfers, Jax must have outranked her. Rebellion stirred in her dagger-sharp eyes.

Taking Yara to the side, Jax whispered in her ear. I strained to hear what they talked about, but the girl started humming the annoying tune that Pixie Swap played when you lost. I knew it well because I lost all the time.

Yara bowed her head and slipped away without another glance toward me.

I was relieved. She made me feel like another Timesurfer was one too many.

"Welcome." Jax turned around and raised his voice to address all three of us. He helped me off the ramp and offered his arm to the girl, who yawned, rubbing her eyes.

"Jennifer, this is Opal." Jax gestured toward the girl. "Her mother, who shall remain nameless by request, is a high-ranking government official who provides our operations with the funds we need for research." He gestured toward the older woman. "This is Opal's nanny."

I offered my hand, but neither of them took it, so I wiped it on my tunic like it was diseased.

"Why is your hair so pale?" Opal stared at me.

The nanny gave me an apologetic smile and whispered in Opal's ear. "That's her true color."

I shifted from foot to foot, feeling like a freak on display. I'd never fit in to this futuristic world, even with the right-looking tunic.

Jax smiled and his sapphire eyes focused on me. "A beautiful color."

Heat rose to my cheeks.

He turned away. "Come, we have much to see."

We followed Jax down a long, gleaming white corridor. Glass windows revealed rooms on either side, equipped with wallscreens and tables, illuminating star charts and other celestial dust clouds and nebulas. People in white coats leaned over the charts, measuring distances with long pointy instruments.

Jax waved his hand like a magician. "Potential star systems yet to be explored. Our scientists work around the clock, compiling data from the latest satellite images. Right now they're plotting the safest and fastest course to Paradise 15."

Opal tugged on the hem of her tunic and turned to her nanny. "I want some chewy tarts."

"Of course, dear." The older woman pulled a wrapper out of her pocket, and Opal snatched it from her fingers.

I shook my head, rolling my eyes when no one looked. This was a poor excuse for a tour group. Good thing I was interested enough to think of questions. "How long do you think it will take to reach Paradise 15?"

Jax raised his eyebrows. "Good question. We're thinking somewhere between two hundred and fifty to two hundred and sixty years, based on the flight speed of a small scout ship." He watched me carefully, perhaps gauging my reaction to see if the number of years scared me.

It didn't. I put both hands on my hips. "For someone who's been frozen for three hundred, it could be worse."

"Of course." He sighed like he'd held his breath.

"When are we going to see the animals?" Opal whined from behind us. Her nanny shushed her.

Animals? They have real animals? Like Martha's cat? Excitement rushed up my legs and zapped my heart. I almost giggled with glee.

Jax crouched down on his knees to meet Opal in the eye. "Very soon, dear." He patted her head and she stuck her tongue out. He responded with a sweet smile and straightened up.

"If you'll follow me…" Jax turned and started down the corridor. Not wanting to get too close to Opal, I walked beside him, letting the girl and her nanny trail behind us.

The scrawled letters spelling *Sophie* peeked out from his rolled-up sleeve in red and blue ink. My eyes kept darting to them, but my lips remained sealed.

Jax stopped along an airtight door and pressed a code into a panel. The sides parted and arctic air rushed out. I grabbed my shoulders, rubbing my hands up and down my arms.

"Don't worry. We won't stay in here long." Jax showed us into a lab. Metal tubes, each big enough to fit a sumo wrestler, lined the walls. He pressed another code into a keypad, and the metal lining twisted away. I expected to see frozen bodies, like in a horror movie, but instead, rows of small glass vials lined the center.

Mist poured from inside the tube as he reached in and pulled out one of the vials. A label lay just beneath his fingertips.

"Amur Leopard?"

"That's right. Here we have DNA for every species to ever have walked the Earth." His blue eyes sparkled as if the cool air had sharpened them. "Even dinosaurs."

Although I was impressed, Opal kicked one of the tubes in the back, making a resonating *thud thud thud* behind us.

I took the vial in my hands. "It seems so fragile."

Jax nodded. "We also have the protein sequences stored on a hard drive, but it will be easier to work with actual cells once we get to Paradise 15."

The thuds grew louder as Opal grew more impatient.

"Opal, honey, don't break anything." Her nanny pulled on her arm.

She yanked away, chewing her candy. "This is boring." She popped the last bite in her mouth and threw the wrapper on the floor.

I thought Jax would do something to scold her, but he smiled smoothly. "Let's get to the animals, shall we?"

We left the cool storage room and took an elevator down three levels. I couldn't imagine how far we'd traveled underneath the city.

Wake up, Jenny. Now was the time to get answers, not daydream and gawk.

I cleared my throat, trying to sound professional. "What species do you plan on bringing back first?"

"We must assess the ecosystem on Paradise 15 and determine which species would thrive. We can't simply bring back African lions without first examining the plant species. Herbivores, such as blue wildebeest, need edible plants to survive in order to feed the carnivores like the lions. It's a complicated web of life that we must work at to get the right balance. It may take generations before whole ecosystems are created."

The elevator beeped, and we stepped into a long walkway with rows of cells on either side.

"Of course, first we have to make sure we *can* bring them back." Jax's lips curled like a secret rested on his tongue. Behind him, I could have sworn I heard a monkey hooting.

Opal pushed by me, and her pigtails whipped the air.

"Opal, wait!" Her nanny cursed under her breath and launched after her.

"Nice kid." I turned to Jax and gave him a sly smile, opening the door for any snide comment of his own.

His face was devoid of any malice. "Her mother is one of our biggest benefactors. Thus, Opal's very important to us. A visit now and then is nothing compared to the political backing we'll have once her mother appeals to Congress on behalf of our cause."

The Timesurfers were very important to Jax. *Willing to suffer anything important.* As important as my dreams were to me.

Jax caught my stare. He raised one eyebrow as if I'd unpeeled a layer of his true self and liked what I saw. "I think you'll appreciate enclosure thirty-three-A the most."

Curiosity ate my composure until my legs itched to run ahead like Opal as I followed Jax to a large set of double doors. Jax input a code, and the panels parted, revealing a meadow the length of my street back home. Long grass and wildflowers grew under simulated sunlight. Bird song lilted in the sweet air, and a sparrow hopped on a nearby branch of a crabapple tree.

Jax spread his arm over the landscape. "A microcosm of the Northeastern grasslands."

A whinny echoed over a hill and seized my heart until my legs felt like mush. I collapsed to the ground, tears blurring my eyes. A horse, white as a unicorn, crested the hill. The mare stared down at us through thick eyelashes.

I gasped in a sob, thinking of Thunderbolt. Had anyone ridden him after I was frozen? Or did he waste away, his muscles growing weaker with each year, waiting for my return? This horse could have been his distant cousin, so sharp was her gaze, as if it stared directly into my soul. If I whispered my regrets to this magnificent creature standing before me, would my message reach through time and touch Thunderbolt?

Jax knelt beside me and took my hand. "Was I wrong to bring you here?"

"No, no, no." I wiped my cheeks with my sleeve. "It's just... I had a horse back when...you know."

"I know." Jax's eyes grew soft as a blue sky. He squeezed my hand in his. "I read it in your profile. You'd be surprised how much is archived from our pasts."

Sniffing up tears, I pushed myself up. My legs wobbled, but Jax held me steady.

"Would you like to get closer?"

"Hell, yeah." I steeled my nerves, trying to bring myself back from the blubbering mess I'd become. Jax walked me up the hill and put his hand on the mare's muzzle. She pushed into his touch, neighing softly. I felt her warm breath on my cheeks.

Jax laughed. "Jennifer, meet Snow."

I reached out and ran my fingers along Snow's neck, the familiar sensation of coarse, dusty hair on my palms. The earthy smell of hide brought fresh tears to my eyes. "It's been so long since I touched one."

This was my dream. In a simulated meadow in a secret facility underneath a skyscraper choked city, I'd finally found what I'd been looking for.

"Wonderful, isn't it?" Jax smiled beside me and suddenly the Timesurfers' plan didn't seem so farfetched. This horse felt more real to me than anything in that strange land of skyscrapers and hover-crafts. "I promise you. We will bring them back."

A scream broke the moment, tearing through my bliss like a knife through a satin sheet. We both turned toward the door and the horse pulled away and galloped down the hill behind us. My chest ached to see the horse leave, but the nanny's look of horror on her red-blotched face stole my attention.

She staggered toward us. "There's been an accident. It's Opal."

"Oh, geez. Where is she?" Jax looked more scared than when we'd hung off the side of the high-rise.

"The monkey room."

Jogging toward the door, Jax pressed a wrist band on his arm and shouted into it, "Medics needed immediately in cell fifty-seven-A."

He disappeared around the corner. Should I stay put or follow? The nanny stared at me like all this was my fault. Maybe it was. I rushed by her, following Jax down the corridor.

My heart hammered in my chest and I wished I'd actually *tried* to run in gym. There were so many cells, each one a different ecosystem. As I ran, I could see blurred trees, furry hides, and bright feathers through the small windows of the different cells. So many things to look at and no time to see any of them.

I reached the door seconds after Jax turned the corner and stopped in my tracks. Vines hung from the ceiling, and a pungent scent of sickly sweet blossoms choked my throat. How big were those monkeys?

I shoved down my fear. *Jax and Opal are in there, and they may need my help.* I ducked underneath the vines and stepped into a jungle. Humidity beaded on my face and palm fronds brushed my legs as I trudged ahead. The leaves grew so thick that I had to brush them back again and again, thorns pricking my arms. A parrot squawked above me, and I jumped back, feeling foolish. The vial with Amur Leopard printed on it surfaced in my memory and I blocked it out. Surely Jax would keep the dangerous animals secured.

I emerged in a clearing with a fancy jungle gym in the center. Opal lay face up on a pile of dirt, her eyes closed. A red welt throbbed on her forehead. Jax knelt beside the girl, feeling her pulse.

I squatted beside him, horrified. "Is she all right?"

"Her pulse is steady. Looks like she got knocked out." He shook his head, "I should have been here supervising."

My face stung with guilt. I'd distracted him. "I'm sorry."

"Don't be sorry. It's my mistake."

The nanny rushed in, wringing her hands. "It all happened so fast."

"*What* happened?" Jax looked around, but the jungle gym was clear. Whatever *had* happened scared all of the monkeys away.

"She was chasing them around and pulling their tails, and all of a sudden one of those little devils fought back. It turned on her, smacking her in the face."

I gritted my teeth, trying to keep my mouth closed. It wasn't the monkey's fault. That was the problem with the world, and in three hundred years it hadn't changed. No one respected nature. People's desires always came first.

"I'll have my medics take her to the emergency center." Jax placed a hand on Opal's forehead.

Men in blue uniforms rushed in behind us carrying a stretcher. One of them nodded to Jax. "We'll take it from here."

One medic lifted Opal onto the stretcher while another attached an oxygen mask to her face and another read vital signs in her eyes.

"Next time we should stick to stuffed animals." The nanny followed them out of the monkey cell, leaving Jax and me alone.

"Are we safe here?"

"Of course we're safe. These monkeys are the size of my foot. She must have really egged them on."

I was worried, not only for Opal, even though I didn't like her, but for Jax and the Timesurfers. It was never good to bite the hand that fed you. "Will she be okay?"

Jax sat cross-legged in the dirt and ran both hands through his hair until it stood up even more than usual. "Yeah, she'll be fine. I'll send a nice package home with her, give her some candy, and with some luck she'll forget it ever happened."

Even though he'd already said it wasn't my fault, guilt still burnt my cheeks. "If it wasn't for me, you would have been here to stop her."

"It's not you. It's just…" His voice trailed off and he covered his face with both hands. I heard a plaintive holler behind us, then silence.

I scanned the ferns around us. Nothing moved. My curiosity won over my fear. I sat beside him and whispered, "What is it, Jax?"

He took in a deep breath, like he needed more air to say it out loud. "She reminds me so much of Sophie."

Sophie? A six-year-old girl? Somehow, I'd pictured her to be a six-foot-tall model with silky auburn hair and very large breasts, wearing a bikini.

My fingertips brushed the tattoo on his arm. I knew if I asked who she was it would change everything. "Sophie?"

"My daughter."

His words stunned me into silence. I knew he had a few years on me, but to already be a father?

"I was born as *Jack* Upton. I changed my name to fit in here. Jennifer, I was frozen too."

I stared at Jax like he was a stranger all over again. "What year?"

He pried his hands off his cheeks and turned to face me. His face had paled, and redness rimmed his eyes. For the first time, he looked vulnerable. "Two-thousand-twenty-three."

"That's impossible. I had our family robot search the cybernet for others like myself..."

"When I joined the Timesurfers, I had my records erased to remain anonymous."

"I didn't know you could do that."

"It's not easy, but the Timesurfers have a lot of resources. You'd be surprised what they can do to keep their own safe."

So many questions buzzed in my mind. I settled for the simplest one. "How old are you, really?"

"I was twenty when I was frozen, and I've been awake now for three years. Time is all relative when you've slept for centuries." He laughed. "In a way, you're older than me because you were frozen longer."

I didn't find his comment funny. "Why didn't you tell me?"

"My life before cryo isn't something I talk about often. This world is so different than the one I left, sometimes whole days go by when I can pretend not to remember."

Jax's voice wavered. What had he left behind? I didn't want to cause him any more pain. "You don't have to tell me."

"No. I should. If anyone will understand, it'll be you."

I swallowed hard, my tongue a dry wad in my mouth. Did I really want to know?

Jax straightened up, leaning back on his palms. He looked off into the canopy of trees. "One day I was flying to visit my grandmother on a Boeing 747, row twelve on the aisle. Hell, I can still taste the grape juice on my tongue. Feel the cool, recycled air coming from the vent above me. The next moment, I woke up in a hospital bed with everyone I knew long gone."

"You're telling me you didn't choose to be frozen?"

Jax scrunched up his rounded nose in disgust. His eyes darkened. "No. Never in a thousand years would I want this. My family couldn't afford it, either. I wouldn't want them spending the money, to tell you the truth. I've done some research. Sophie's mother invested in the cryosleep process after the crash." He shook his head, the corner of his eyes crinkling. "We fought so much. I thought she hated me."

Jax dug a hole in the dirt with his boot. "Sadie. That was her name. Either she loved me, or she wanted Sophie to have someone in case something happened to her. Still, to this day, I'm not sure."

"Geez, I thought my life was screwed up."

"You're telling me. Imagine being taken in by your daughter's descendants, finding out she grew up without you."

I couldn't imagine it. It was too awful. I couldn't be there for my parents and my brother, but Jax couldn't be there for the one person who needed him the most. What if my dad had been frozen? I would have missed him for the rest of my life, maybe even been angry at him for not being there when I needed him the most. Everyone I talked to had a story worse than mine. It was stupid for me to feel sorry for myself. "Jax, I'm so sorry."

He waved my apology away. "I figured I'd have to tell you sometime if you joined."

A voice buzzed from a keypad on his wrist. "Jax?"

"Yeah, I'm here."

"We need you in the loading bay. Potential donors." The voice fizzled out.

Jax sighed and clicked a button on the side. "I'll be right there."

He stood and brushed the dirt off his black jumpsuit. An apologetic look softened his face. "You *will* join us, won't you? All this hasn't scared you away?"

I rose up, my legs aching after my impromptu run. "No. It's only made me more sure. I know I'm meant to be here to give these animals a second chance."

Jax nodded and smiled. "I knew I could count on you. Come on, I'll show you to your hovercraft."

As we left the jungle, one question still remained on my mind. I gathered my courage and spit it out before I could take it back. "Have they chosen the team for the mission to Paradise 15?"

Jax turned toward me with intensity in his eyes. "No. When they do, you'll know."

CHAPTER TWENTY-FIVE

Surprise

I sat alone on the hovercraft as it lifted from the bay and the panels screeched open above. Cluttered thoughts raced through my mind. I felt like I'd just eaten the biggest meal of my life and now my stomach had to digest it bite by bite. Jax stood below the sight panel, his hand raised as he watched me leave.

Did I want to be on the team?

Yara had called me a great candidate despite her apparent disdain for me, and Jax's intense response—*when they do, you'll know*—made it seem like I was a shoo-in. I knew I wanted in with the Timesurfers, but was deep-space expedition the right place for me? Maybe I was better tending to the animals they had brought back, or just being a donor and visiting from above.

A kernel of anger hardened inside me. That was my fear of cryosleep talking. That wasn't the Jenny who wanted to travel on safari or journey across the arctic glaciers. I used to be so brave. Being frozen had turned me into a coward, stripped away everything I knew. It changed every aspect of my life, and I'd have to do it all over again. I'd lose everyone I'd gotten to know, gotten to care for—Valex, Pell, and Len. Maxim. Only this time, I'd do it by choice.

Heartache zapped my chest when Maxim's name crossed my mind. He wasn't mine, though. He had dreams of his own, and all I'd do is get in the way. Still, my skin tingled when I thought of our kiss. Besides petting Snow, it was the one perfect moment I'd had in this new, crazy world. I couldn't ignore my feelings, but I couldn't act on them, either.

Then there was Jax. He had really opened up to me in the jungle cell, but our pasts drove a wedge between us as much as they bonded us together. A deceased girlfriend who bought his unwanted cryosleep, a long-lost daughter he never saw grow up. That was some serious baggage, even if we were just going to be friends or coworkers. Besides, he'd thought of me as a potential coworker, a great representative for the team. Not a love interest. Jax and me— that was absurd.

I needed some serious time to think. When the hovercraft pulled up to the platform, I felt like I'd stepped back into the world too soon. Dragging my feet to Valex and Len's apartment, I reminded myself that they thought I'd been studying in the library with Maxim. Too solemn a face would give me away.

The doors parted into the walls and a chorus of "Surprise" rang out. I fell back into the hallway as streamers flew at my face. Pell jumped up and down next to another girl with curly brown hair and a clear tube running from her mouth to a small machine on her back. Valex and Len stood behind them with wide grins, holding noisemakers and polka-dotted party hats.

Pell jumped in front of me and grabbed my hand. "Come in, Jennifer. It's our birthday party."

Streamers hung from wall to wall like a giant jellyfish was swimming above my head. Presents stood in a heap in the center next to a pink-frosted birthday cake I could smell from the doorway. I had to remind myself the sweet, strawberry smell was probably artificial, and the cake was probably made of more of that soycrap.

"Jennifer, meet Rainy." Pell brought my hand to her friend's delicate little fingers. I knelt down in front of her and looked into her green-flecked eyes, shaking her hand gently. So beautiful. She looked like Angela's mini-me.

Guilt trickled through me like cold rain. I'd almost gotten in the way of Maxim and Exara. I'd almost left her homeless. No way could such a fragile-looking kid survive in those mold-choked lower levels with the crazies roaming around.

I shook her hand. "Nice to meet you, Rainy. You have pretty eyes."

She giggled as she balanced on one foot, the other scraping the carpet with a yellow shoe. Her nebulizer hummed behind her in a low drone.

I wanted to hug her so bad, but I knew little kids were freaked out by strangers, so I let go of her hand and kept my arms by my sides. "Are you having fun?"

Maxim's sister stared at me with big, blinking eyes.

"Rainy doesn't like to talk." Pell answered for her. "She has to take the breathing piece out of her mouth."

"Oh, I see." I winked at her as I stood up. "Thanks for coming to the party."

Pell turned on Pixie Swap on the wallscreen and Rainy jumped up and down.

"Next one who wins gets the first piece of cake." Pell shouted as the pixies twirled on their lily pads. The two girls began another round.

"I hope you don't mind we combined your birthdays together." Len approached me from the other side of the couch, offering me a party hat.

I took the hat, feeling the cheap plastic bend under my fingers. "'Course not." In fact, I wished they hadn't celebrated mine at all. Rainy and Pell reminded me of Timmy and how I had missed so many of his birthdays. My heart felt like a paper in a shredder. Except, they didn't have paper any more.

Valex came over with a present the size of my miniscreen, wrapped in purple nylon and tied with a shimmery bow. "We got you something."

I'd never had a chance to ask Pell what it was. "You didn't have to." At three hundred and twenty, I was too old for birthday parties. Still, I strapped the hat on and played along.

"We wanted to." Len put her arm around Valex as he held out the present.

I had to take it. Anything else would be rude. "Thank you."

"Open it." Valex encouraged me with a smile.

I ran my hands over the smooth wrapping, feeling a hard binding underneath. At least it wasn't another ugly tunic.

Carefully, I untied the bow. The wrapping slipped off onto the floor, revealing a thick, hardcover leather book with golden binding, like something you'd find in a medieval castle.

It was the first book I'd held in my hands since being frozen. All my homework and reading was done on my miniscreen. The realness of the cover and the weight of it in my arms felt so good. "I didn't think they had books anymore."

"Open the cover." Len nudged me with a gentle hand.

The book opened to a title page that read *Streetwater Family Tree*. I flipped through pages of pictures and names dating back to the eighteen-hundreds. Gertrude Streetwater had worked in the mills on the Merrimack River and her son, Milford, had started a shoe-repair business. There was a chapter on my family, and my finger brushed over a picture of my mom as mayor, cutting the ribbon in front of a new building with Dad standing by her side. Other pictures showed my dad at his massive mahogany desk, Timmy accepting his high-school diploma, and a newly established law firm with the title *Streetwater and Son*. Through the pictures I met Timmy's wife and his two children, a boy with reddish-blond hair and a girl with straight straw-blonde hair like mine. My breath caught in my throat as I read the inscription underneath her baby picture. Timmy had named her Jennifer May after me.

The book filled a small part of the giant hole of oblivion inside me, making me feel partially whole again. "This is wonderful." My voice cracked, and I forced myself not to cry. It would upset Pell, and I didn't want to ruin her birthday.

"It was Len's idea." Valex put his arm around his wife and they looked into each other's eyes, proud of their choice.

Len gave me a sympathetic smile. "We knew we couldn't buy you what you really wanted, so we opted for the closest thing to it."

Valex reached out and flipped a chunk of pages. "It's an old family heirloom. Turn to page four hundred sixty-seven. We've made our own additions."

My fingers shook slightly as I found the page. Valex and Len stood on the roof of a building underneath an arbor, the wind trailing Len's veil behind her white dress. "This is your wedding photo?"

Len nodded. "We wanted you to see how connected to us you are, and that we're not strangers but an offshoot of your immediate family."

"We're more than that." Valex interrupted. "We *are* your immediate family now." A month ago, he would have sounded pushy, but after spending time with them, I kinda liked the idea.

Standing in front of Valex and Len, holding that family tree album, I realized what they really wanted was my love and happiness.

"Thank you." I placed the album on the couch and rushed toward them. Wrapping my arms around both of them, I squeezed hard. It was the first time I felt like we were a real family.

Valex pulled away with watery eyes. "Ready to watch the entire twentieth year of *National Geographic*?"

I pulled back, "You didn't!"

Len laughed, wiping her eyes. "We did. It took hours of searching the archives."

Releasing them, I glanced at a dancing pixie on the screen. "Maybe after their next round. I wouldn't want to interrupt."

"Of course." Len moved toward the kitchen. "I'll get the knife and plates for cake."

Valex moved to help her, but I grabbed his arm. "Hey."

"Yeah?" He stood with his usual casual ease, like the world was everything it should be.

Before, his sunny ambivalence had annoyed me, but now I liked how he worked with what he had, taking my dad's law firm into the next century. His carefree nature came from Timmy. How could I be angry with him for who he was? "I know I haven't been the perfect daughter."

Valex waved my concerns away. "Come on Jenny, that's not true. You've been a great sister to Pell. Look at her; she loves you."

"That was easy. She's such a bright little girl." I smiled and waved at her from across the room.

But I didn't want to talk about Pell. I hardened my resolve. It wasn't easy for me to bring up heavy topics, but I might not have another chance like this. "I mean to you and Len. I was so set on *not* wanting you to replace my parents."

He placed his hand on my shoulder. "That's only natural. We know we can never replace what you had. Len and I just want the best for you. We're here if you need us. But you're a strong young lady, and it seems you don't need us much at all. You're doing just fine on your own."

Was I? I felt like I'd stumbled my way through this strange future. His confidence in me gave me hope.

Len called to him from the kitchen, and Valex squeezed my shoulder. "I have full faith that you will find your way in this world." He walked to the kitchen, and I stood in place in awe of his conviction.

Taking a seat on the couch, I opened the album and flipped back to the pages dedicated to my mom and dad. Their wedding picture, one I remembered hanging over the fireplace, was on the first page. They looked so young and brave in that frozen moment, ready to conquer the world. Mom leaned on Dad's arm like he was her pillar. Dad wore a white tuxedo, a pink rose in his breast pocket. I often wondered who took the picture and what they were thinking at the time.

My chest tightened. Underneath their names was written *John and Lisa Streetwater, born nineteen-sixty and nineteen-sixty-three. Died two-thousand-seventeen.*

My stomach clutched as I fought for breath. Sweat broke out over my head and I felt feverish all at once. They died in the same year. Five years after I was frozen.

CHAPTER TWENTY-SIX

Visitor

Waves of sickening unease spread through my gut as Valex cut the cake. I forced a smile as Len handed me a plate with a huge piece of cake and a spork. They were trying so hard to make me feel included. I couldn't let them know how much their gift upset me. They hadn't meant to scare me, only to show me our connection through time.

Pell nestled up close to me on the couch, her little knee pushing into my thigh, and Rainy sat on my other side, pulling out her mouthpiece to bite into a piece of cake. I couldn't ruin Pell's birthday party over something that happened hundreds of years ago.

"Try some cake, Jennifer." Pell had already smudged pink frosting all over her cheeks, and there was a giant glob on her nose.

My stomach flipped as I brought a small sporkful up to my mouth. No matter what I did today, I couldn't fix whatever had happened. That didn't stop me from itching to run to my miniscreen in my room and scour the archives to dig up information. I'd told myself I wouldn't watch the rest of the discs.

The too-sweet, artificial taste of strawberries sickened my stomach. Had my parents been murdered, or even assassinated? I shoved down the thought as I swallowed.

The worst part was I blamed myself. Somehow, I thought, if I had been awake, I could have prevented their untimely deaths by altering the course of time. The thought was so ridiculous, yet I hung onto it, imagining myself traveling back in time to push them away from a crazed gunman's rifle or a terrorist's bomb.

After I managed to shove down most of the soycake, someone buzzed the door.

Rainy jumped up and shook her head. Pell shouted. "Awww, not yet. We've just started."

Len put a gentle hand on Pell's shoulder. "You know Rainy can't stay out long. The oxygen tank needs to be refilled every few hours."

The doors parted and Maxim stood in my living room, staring at me wearing my polka-dotted party hat, with a sporkful of pink cake hanging in front of my mouth. If I wasn't so freaked out about my parents, I would have been mortified.

"Hello, Mr. and Mrs. Streetwater, Rainy, Pell…" His voice changed on my name, growing deeper. "Jenny."

"Fifteen more minutes." Pell tugged on Len's silver tunic. "Just one more round of Pixie Swap."

Len gave Maxim a questioning look and he nodded. "I'm in no rush. Go ahead."

"Yay!" Pell jumped up and down and cake crumbs flew all over the floor. C-7 had his work cut out for him tomorrow.

Maxim rounded the couch and sat next to me. Len handed him a piece of cake. "Thanks for staying awhile."

"No problem. Thanks for the cake." Maxim dove right in as if he hadn't eaten all day. He watched his sister and smiled. Unconditional love filled his eyes, and I wanted both of them to be safe in their high-rise forever.

Len and Valex retreated to the kitchen to help C-7 clean up, leaving me alone with Maxim as Pell and Rainy played Pixie Swap on the floor in front of the wallscreen.

Maxim gave me a tentative smile. "I didn't know it was your birthday, too."

I shrugged, my emotions spiking and falling like tidal waves. "Knowing how old I really am, I tried to keep it under wraps." I'd give the Crypt Keeper a run for his money.

"If I'd known, I would've brought you something."

"You can't give me what I really want." My breath caught as I choked on a piece of cake. Did I really just say that out loud?

Maxim's eyebrows shot up. I'd stunned him into silence. He turned away, his shoulders slumping and his dark hair falling in his eyes.

"I'm sorry. I don't know what's gotten into me today. Everything was going well. Valex and Len gave me this family album, which is more than sweet."

He swallowed hard and put his plate down on the arm of the couch. In front of us, Pell and Rainy cried out in triumph. His eyes met mine. "So what's wrong, Jenny?"

I felt I could tell him anything, and I needed someone to talk to. Valex and Len would only feel bad that their present had stirred up the past. Maxim had been my confidant all along. I could trust him.

I flicked my gaze over to the kitchen. How long did we have? Our conversations always seemed stolen, rushed into the cracks of life. Dishes clanged as C-7 loaded the tray and Valex and Len talked loudly about how successful the party was. Pell sang the winning-pixie tune, so they couldn't hear me even if I shouted. I had a few minutes, at most.

Leaning in close to Maxim, I whispered, "I found my parent's dates in the book. When they were born…and when…" I squeezed my eyes shut as if I could block it out. "When they died."

"That's awful." Maxim put his hand on my arm and shook his head. "You shouldn't have to see that." He cast a glance over his shoulder. "What were they thinking?"

"They only wanted to help, to show me we were connected in some way. It's not their fault."

"I'm sorry." He squeezed my arm with his rough, callused hands. "I wish you hadn't seen that on your birthday."

"It gets worse." I breathed in deeply. "My parents died in the same year, only five years after I was frozen."

"What happened?"

I shook my head. "The album doesn't say."

Maxim pursed his lips. He studied me with a solemn hesitation in his eyes. "Do you really want to know?"

Biting my lip, I nodded. "It's the only way I can find closure. I *need* to know what happened."

"Then we'll scour the archives, look for anything—"

I caught Maxim's hand, interrupting him. "I have a better way."

CHAPTER TWENTY-SEVEN

Truths

Maxim checked Rainy's nebulizer levels. Red digital numbers flashed on a small screen behind her head. Rainy swatted at him, but he hovered out of reach.

"Leave her alone, bothead." Pell stuck out her tongue.

I gave Pell a stern look. "He's making sure Rainy can stay longer."

Maxim ignored the girls and glanced back at me, his eyes intense. "We have time."

Time was only half the problem, but I didn't want to face the truth alone.

We walked into the kitchen and I scrounged up my courage. Valex and Len were reviewing birthday pictures on their camera. They looked up at me and Maxim with wary frowns.

"We have to finish a school project, so we're going to my room where it's quiet."

"Doesn't Rainy have to go home?" Len's voice was soft, careful.

"Rainy's good for another hour or so." Maxim leaned against the countertop, looking suave, like he asked to go into girls' bedrooms all the time. "Plus, she wants to stay."

"Can't you study in the living room?" Len pressed, her fingers turning white as she tightened her grip on the camera.

As if to illustrate my dilemma, Pell shrieked and Rainy clapped as Pixie Swap's winning tune blasted behind us again. I gave Len a pleading stare. It was my birthday, after all. If you didn't count the years I was frozen, I was eighteen, and I didn't need their permission. Though it *was* their apartment.

"Oh, all right." Len quirked an eyebrow in warning. "Don't dally for too long."

In any other circumstance, I'd have been giddily nervous to take him to my room, but my parents' mysterious deaths hung over me like a shroud. I'd gone from dreading truth to seeking it, and the complete one-eighty left me feeling the universe had chewed my heart up and spit it out.

I wished I'd taken the time to fold my rumpled tunics. Maxim stepped over my clothes like he didn't even notice the tragic state of my room and glanced at the recycling chute. "Up there?"

"Yup." I stepped beside him, kicking away stray socks. "We'll have to climb on my bed, and you'll have to lift me."

"Cyberhell, Jenny, why you'd make it so hard?"

"Because I didn't want to be tempted to watch the videos. I didn't want to know."

He gave me an overprotective look. "Now you want to know?"

I sighed in exasperation. Every second counted. "Yes."

"Okay. But if your guardians catch me on your bed holding you up, I'm done for."

The corner of my lips curled. "They never come in here. Now get up there and hoist me up." I'd shoved the discs so far back that it would keep me from watching them when temptation hit.

He slipped off his shoes and climbed on my bed, looking like a surfer riding an especially unpredictable wave. I summoned my courage and jumped up to join him.

"Ready?" His breath touched my cheek.

"Ready."

Maxim wrapped strong hands around my waist and hefted me up. I reached over my head and felt for the discs. Dust wafted down and I sneezed.

"Can you feel them?"

"I think so." My fingertips brushed a hard plastic case. "Just a little higher."

Maxim stretched his arms and I swiped my arm across the chute. The discs tumbled out all over my bed, some of them hitting us in the head.

"Ah! You could have warned me." Maxim sniffed. "I just swallowed a dust bunny."

"And I thought you were all vegetarians in the future." I double-checked with my arm to make sure I hadn't left any behind. "Got 'em all."

Maxim lowered me. "Good. I don't think I could stomach another round."

We climbed off the bed.

"Look for twenty-eight through thirty-one."

Maxim coughed like a cat hacking up a hairball. "Yes, ma'am."

We dug through the pile and I checked for any that might have fallen under the bed.

He dusted one off and discarded it over his shoulder. "Nope. Eighteen. Why'd you stop at twenty-eight, anyway?"

The truth punched me in the gut. "I didn't want to accept the fact that my family moved on without me."

Maxim put his hand on my shoulder, and I had to resist leaning into his touch, accepting his sympathy, drowning the hurt in his warmth. It would be so easy to rub against him, fall on top of him, press my lips against his…

Blinking back my raging hormones, I flung up two discs. "Here are thirty and thirty-one."

It didn't take long to find the other two. I clicked on my wallscreen and Maxim held the disc in front of the drive. "Are you sure?"

I nodded, afraid if I spoke, my voice would break.

Maxim popped the disc in and joined me on my bed.

A narrator's voice echoed in my room. "This is the journey of the dwindling population of polar bears on Earth…" The scene panned out from a shrinking glacier to the vastness of the ocean.

"What the—"

"Try the next disc." I handed him disc twenty-nine.

Sure enough, after Maxim popped the disc in, Angela came on the screen holding a baby in her arms. She looked older, her body a little more filled out, with tired wrinkles around her eyes. "Jenny,

I'm so sorry I haven't talked to you in so long. I've been busy." She flashed that all-knowing, secret smile I knew so well, and the old Angela came back for a second. "I want you to meet the newest member of our family, baby Todd."

"Who's that?" Maxim whispered.

I froze up. Should I tell him the truth? What would he think of me after knowing I'd been best friends with his great-great-great-grandmother? I didn't want to weird him out, but at the same time, he'd done so much for me that I thought he deserved a decent answer.

"That's my best friend, Angela." I wrapped a thread from my blanket around my finger so tightly the tip turned red. "She's also your ancestor."

Maxim shook his head like he hadn't heard me correctly. "What?"

I had to tell him everything. While baby Todd cried in the background, my mind traveled back to that fateful day I forgot my shoes in gym. "I had a crush on this guy named Chad."

Maxim crossed his arms like he didn't like hearing about Chad one bit. "And?"

"After I was frozen, my best friend dated him. They went to prom together and eventually got married. At first I felt betrayed, but now I'm glad she found someone to love. Anyway, when I watched the videos, I realized something."

I looked down, wrapping the thread tighter. "There's always been something about you that I was drawn to. Something familiar, something I liked. I couldn't put my finger on it at first, but then one day Angela's face froze on my wallscreen." I reached out and touched his dark hair where it curled against his neck. "You have the same hair as Angela."

Maxim's lips tightened in denial. "That doesn't mean anything. There are thousands of people with this type of hair."

I raised my finger to silence him. "I had C-7 go back through your family tree. Maxim, my best friend and the boy I liked were your ancestors."

Maxim rubbed his hands over his face, stretching his cheeks out. He tangled his fingers in his hair and held them there. Spiky clumps stuck out between his fingers. "What does that make us?"

I knew it. Freak-out time. I took a deep breath. "If anything, it brings us closer. I loved my best friend. When I look at you, I see everything I liked about her."

"Isn't it messed up? I mean, you kissed me." Maxim furrowed his eyebrows until his forehead was a bunch of wrinkles. "Isn't that like kissing your best friend?"

"At first I didn't know what to think, but then I realized the connection just made me like you more." My cheeks burned with the truth.

He sat back against the wall, and I felt guilty for not telling him sooner. "I didn't want to tell you because I didn't want to scare you away."

"You'd never scare me away, Jenny."

So what? He'd just lurk on the edge of my sight, teasing me every day of my life? Frustration built up like lava inside me. "Look, it doesn't matter anyway. We're not supposed to be together, right? You have your responsibilities."

Angela's disc stopped and the screen turned blank. "Let's just get this over with and pop in the next disc."

Unwilling to argue, I got up, ejected Angela's disc, and popped in the second to last one, hoping it wasn't more polar bears or messages from my best friend.

Crashing waves stretched out on my wallscreen above a white railing. Mom leaned against the side, her hair blowing in the wind. She laughed as the camera turned on Dad's face. He wore a Hawaiian shirt and carried a margarita with an orange umbrella.

Maxim's face instantly softened. "Is that them?"

"Yeah." My heart broke all over again as they twirled across the deck. "This must be an old vacation video someone threw in."

"Do you want to keep watching?"

As much as the sight of my parents together, healthy and happy, comforted me, I needed to know the truth. "Fast forward. See if there's anything else."

After a luau with fire dancers and a walk along a sandy beach, the video faded out.

Maxim held up the last disc. "Just one left."

Maybe there was no answer on the discs after all. For all I knew, this last one could be another vacation video or another season of *National Geographic*. I felt stupid for bringing Maxim here, for making him sit through old family movies. "Maybe I was wrong."

"We have to give it a try." Maxim stuck the disc in and sat beside me on the bed. We waited, my heart beating faster each second as the wallscreen read the old disc.

Timmy's adult face stared back at me, darkness tingeing the corners of his eyes. "Hi, Jenny." Standing in Dad's study, he wore a black suit with a long black tie, and the solemn tone of his outfit took the breath right out of me. The white lilies in the back screamed funeral.

Timmy let out a heavy sigh. "This will be the last entry in my video collection to you. I know I haven't kept up with it, but life has gotten in the way, and to tell you the truth, I've spent so many hours waiting." He rubbed his forehead like he had a headache. "I need to move on."

Beside me, Maxim threaded his fingers through mine. I held on, glad he was there.

Loosening his tie, Timmy angled the camera so he could sit down at my dad's mahogany desk. He picked up Dad's paperweight, a golden globe of Earth, and ran his fingers along the impressions in the surface. "I considered leaving it be, but if you ever wake up one day, I want you to know what happened to Mom and Dad."

My heart leapt to my throat and I struggled to breathe. My chest felt like a python had squeezed around it. Maxim tightened his grip beside me.

"I was at school when it happened." Timmy rubbed his eyes, almost looking as though he'd changed his mind and would shut off the video before I had a chance to learn the truth. I leaned forward, my eyes glued to the wallscreen. *Please, Timmy, I need to know.*

"It was their anniversary. They were driving on route 102 to Luigi's when an old Chevy hydroplaned and hit them head-on. They're gone, Jenny. Just like you. I couldn't freeze them. The coroner said after the fire there wasn't enough left.

"I've decided I don't want to be frozen, no matter what happens to me. The doctors promised Mom and Dad that they were close, but now they're saying they're nowhere near a cure. Who knows if we'd even wake up in the same decade? Besides, I've met someone, a woman I can't live without. We're going to get married after I graduate, and I want to be by her side forever, even if it means I go with her in this lifetime. Jenny, I'm sorry. I always thought we'd be together, and I've loved you forever, but I need to let you go."

The video clicked off and the screen went as black as the hole in my chest. I'd lost them all over again. Somehow knowing my parents' lives had been cut short, while mine had been prolonged, made it worse. They'd had so many plans, so many hopes and dreams. Dad wanted to expand his business. Mom always said she'd retire early and finally have time to spend with us. Their untimely deaths made me realize that I had to live my dreams now. You never knew how much time you really had.

Maxim held me as my body convulsed with sobs. He wrapped me in his arms and I let the sorrow overtake me in an inevitable tidal wave.

CHAPTER TWENTY-EIGHT

Hope

"You sure you'll be okay, Jennifer?" Len touched the back of my hand as I lay curled in a ball on the couch. She slung her miniscreen bag across her pressed navy tunic, looking like the perfect futuristic businesswoman.

Wrapped up in a formless robe, I felt like such a slouch. "Yeah, I just need some time to myself. To sort things out."

"Take all the time you need. I've let Principal Hall know you'll be out for a while."

"Thanks, Len." She and Valex had been very understanding when I told them about the final video. I made sure not to mention anything about the album, so they thought I had just turned it on to be close to my family for my birthday.

Len touched her bag. "Buzz my miniscreen if you need me."

I nodded.

Len hugged Pell and slipped out the front door. Valex had already left, and C-7 buzzed in the kitchen, cleaning.

Pell ran over and kissed my cheek, "Feel better soon."

"Thanks, kiddo. Sorry you have to ride the bus alone."

"It's okay. I'm a big girl now." Ever since her birthday party, Len and Valex had been feeding her that phrase to get her to do "big girl" things. I was surprised it worked.

"You are." I tousled her hair. "Kick some cyber butt in school today."

"I always get straight A's." Pell grabbed her lunch container and scampered out of the apartment, leaving me with C-7. A while back, I would have been afraid to be alone with him, but now I was glad for his company, even if he *was* a robot.

Minutes after everyone left, C-7's metal feet clicked on the linoleum. The steps grew silent as he reached the carpeted living room. I glanced up. He still wore his apron from cleaning the dishes, and a towel dangled from his silver fingers.

I straightened up, thinking he needed me to get up to wipe down the couch, but he didn't move. "Something wrong?"

"Jennifer, your miniscreen is beeping with a message."

I blinked, wondering how he had access to my incoming mail. Was he all-knowing like HAL from *2001*? Maybe he'd just cleaned my room and saw it blinking.

"I'll check it later. I don't want to get up." It was probably Maxim worrying about me, or Principal Hall sending his condolences. Right now I didn't want to deal with either of them.

He titled his oblong head and his eye seemed to wink in the glint of fluorescent light. "This message might cheer you up."

"Oh, all right." I pulled myself up, my muscles creaking. Collecting the tail of my robe in my arms, I dragged my feet to my room.

I squashed down hope as I flipped open the lid. Who could it possibly be to cheer me up? My parents and Timmy were gone, and Maxim was still with Exara. Nothing could change the absolutes in my life.

Jax's face flashed on, eagerness etched in his boyishly round features. I started to shake all over. This could only mean one thing.

"Congratulations, Jennifer. You've made the team." A smile worked its way onto his lips before he put on a serious face. "It will be you, me, Yara, and two others whom you haven't met. We leave this Friday, November twenty-sixth, at precisely eight-thirty-five PM. A hovercraft will pick you up at eleven-twenty-one AM so you can start the initiation process. Pack only what you can carry on your back. A lawyer will be available to carry out any last wishes on your behalf. Of course, secrecy is needed for this mission to take off as planned. No one can know about your impending departure.

Buzz this number if you have any questions or if you change your mind."

The message flickered out, leaving me stunned.

Me? Chosen for an intergalactic space mission to Paradise 15? Deep down I'd known this could happen, but the reality of it struck me like a lightning bolt and I couldn't move.

Did I want to go? I had felt complete wholeness when I touched that horse. The yearning to ride surged up inside me. This futuristic high-rise world suffocated me. If I stayed, I'd end up like Martha. In my heart of hearts I knew the answer. *Yes.*

Was it the best path? Valex and Len had their own lives, and soon Pell would grow up and find a job and spouse. If I stayed, I could visit with them from time to time, but I couldn't build my life around theirs. I couldn't live my life for them.

What about Maxim? My heart shuddered as I thought of leaving him behind. Living a life of stolen kisses and secret conversations wasn't enough for me. If I bought his family's high-rise, I'd feel I was buying his love. The last thing I wanted was for Maxim to feel chained to me like he did Exara. Knowing him, he wouldn't take my money anyway.

I brought up the calendar on my miniscreen and double-checked the date—Monday, November 22. The mission left on Friday. Four days to prepare. Four days to change my mind.

I slipped on a long-sleeved tunic sweater and velcroed up my thigh-high boots. The air had winter's chilly edge to it, but I wouldn't be around for Christmas.

"Where are you going, Jennifer?" C-7 met me as I tried to slip out the door. I had a few hours at most before Pell got home.

I clutched my backpack with shaking hands and stared him down, daring him to stop me. "I have to visit someone."

C-7 moved toward me and my heart sped up. Would he physically hold me back? He raised his arm and I shrank back against the wall. This was it. My life would end with a murderous robot crushing my skull.

He placed a gentle hand on my shoulder, and shame for my prejudices tingled in my face. "Make sure you're back before two forty-five."

I stared into his unchanging, twilight eyes. "Why are you helping me?"

His head tilted and gears buzzed underneath a panel in his neck. "Because you need it."

"But, I mean, you could get into a lot of trouble. You told me before you could have your memory erased. Why risk so much?"

There was a dent in his arm, a chink in his robotic armor. What had caused it? Was it like a scar? All of a sudden he looked more vulnerable.

C-7's voice spoke softly, with a slight change in intonation. "I know what it is like to be misunderstood."

All those times Pell yelled at him and called him bothead came to mind. All C-7 did was help, and Valex and Len took him for granted while their daughter hated him. I was the only one who ever noticed him, who ever talked to him like a person. In a way, I was his only friend.

"Thanks. You're a big help." Without him, I wouldn't have found Martha in the first place, or been introduced to the Timesurfers.

C-7 turned away, dusting a cranny in the wall. "You should go."

I checked the time on the wallscreen. "You're right. I have a few hours at most."

As I turned to leave, C-7's voice held me still. "Life is a gamble, but nothing worth having is not without some form of risk."

Only when I got on the hoverbus did I realize he wasn't talking about going out today. He was talking about going on the mission.

C-7 knew.

"Come back for more, tea, eh?" Martha winked as I stepped into her apartment.

"Um…sure." I couldn't tell her why I was there. Jax had clearly instructed me not to tell anyone about the mission. Still, I couldn't leave without saying good-bye in some way.

Jumbo pounced on the floor in front of me and hissed.

"Yeah, it's good to see you, too."

"Don't mind him." Martha puttered around in the kitchen. Porcelain cups rattled. "The old geezer has indigestion problems that are making him snippy."

I swallowed hard. "Is he going to be okay?" There was a bald spot on his back I hadn't noticed before.

"He's sixteen years old. That's eighty in people years."

The thought of Martha's cat dying and leaving her alone made me sick. I wished I could take her with me. "I joined the Timesurfers, Martha."

Her eyes gleamed as she brought in two cups of steaming tea. "I knew you would. Did they show you their underground base?"

"Oh, yeah." I thought back to the animals as I took my cup and balanced it on my legs. "I got to touch a real horse."

"Miraculous, isn't it?" Martha settled beside me on the couch.

I swirled the tea around with a tiny spoon. "And their plans for the future..."

She nodded, her wispy purple-gray hair like a cloud on her head. "Scouting for planets to start over. Just the thought fills an old lady like me with hope."

"I'm sure they'd enjoy your visit."

"Nah... I'm too old to help with anything, I'd just be a burden. Besides, I couldn't leave Jumbo alone. He'd tear up my antique couch with separation anxiety."

I ran my fingers over an elaborate snowflake-patterned doily on the armrest. "Can't have that."

"No. You go. Find out all you can. Help them bring back animals so Jumbo can have a friend."

It was an empty hope, like talking to someone with a life sentence about the vacation they'd take to Hawaii if they could. The time it would take to travel to Paradise 15, inhabit it, set up laboratories, and birth new species was way beyond Jumbo's almost-spent lifetime. Still, I played along. "He'd probably claw their eyes out."

Martha laughed and her tea rippled in the cup. "Only until he got to know them."

We sat in silence for a few minutes, Jumbo rubbing against the wall. I ran my finger over the golden rim of my teacup, feeling a chip in the porcelain under my skin. "Thank you for telling me about the Timesurfers. I know it could have put you in danger…"

"Nonsense. You're a special girl, Jennifer. I knew from the moment you walked in here you were destined for greatness."

"I don't know about that. More like destined for clumsiness."

We laughed together, her sipping her tea and me lifting the cup up to my lips and pretending. She'd changed from a miserly skeptic to a sweet old lady in the short time I had known her, and I wondered how much of that change was because of me. I might have been over-crediting myself, but still I didn't want her thinking I abandoned her. "I'm not going to be able to visit you anymore. I can't say why, but I want you to know it's not because I don't want to."

Martha sighed and her frail shoulders slumped forward. "I had an inkling. There's an eagerness in your eyes, like a child at Christmastime."

If only I could tell her about my upcoming adventure. I didn't want to endanger her with information people would kill for. It wasn't like Martha would tell anyone except for Jumbo, but who knew what devices they had these days for listening in on conversations?

I checked the time on my miniscreen. Pell would be home in less than an hour. I took a long gulp of bitter tea and stood up. "I'm sorry. I have to go."

Martha placed her cup on the armrest and struggled to get up. "Oh, these old bones…" She walked over and gave me a hug. I held onto her, missing my grandmother.

She pulled away and wiped at a stain on the couch that must have been there for the last forty years. "Maybe my second chance wasn't for nothing. Maybe I was supposed to be here to tell you about the Timesurfers so you could go on and do the work I wanted to do."

The urge to tell her welled up inside me, and I tightened my lips and wiped my eyes. "I'll certainly try."

I looked back one more time.

Martha winked, a sparkle in her eyes. "Have a safe trip."

CHAPTER TWENTY-NINE

Last Day

The cold froze the marrow of my bones, and stillness held my soul until I couldn't remember what it was like to feel the sun on my skin, or the heat trapped under a blanket. All I saw was the curved lid of the cryotube through a glassy substance that could only be preservation liquid.

Wait a second. I'm supposed to be asleep.

Panic filled my throat. I tried to scream, but my breath wouldn't release. My lungs were full to bursting, yet at the same time a suffocating feeling of drowning came over me. This wasn't like the last time I went under. I lay encased and alone, fully aware but unable to move. Numbness tingled through me and I couldn't hear, feel, or touch. Only stare at the tiny crystals in the liquid and, through them, the lid. Only think.

My thoughts raced. Would I suffer like this for the next two hundred and fifty years? Imprisoned with only my thoughts to keep me company? No! I'd go crazy without a way to sense the passing of time, with no visual stimulus to keep me distracted.

I wanted to crack the ice and break through the frozen liquid to claw at the underside of the lid. Anything to get out into the fresh air. To breathe again. Maybe the ship hadn't taken off, and I could get someone's attention.

My mind pushed against a brick wall as I struggled to move. Light flickered above me. The lid had a triangular box of clear glass just above my head. Faces stared down at me, middle-aged men with the cold, clinical eyes of scientists. I screamed my thoughts at them. Their lips moved and I made out the words. Procedure successful. Or maybe it was my imagination telling me my greatest fear.

Fingers tapped on the glass and the men disappeared, leaving me staring at nothing as the light flickered out.

I bolted upright in bed, shivering so hard my teeth hurt. What day was it? How long had I been out? My muscles ached and my bones creaked like my real three-hundred-year age had finally caught up to me. It seemed I'd been asleep for centuries, but when I checked my miniscreen, it was Thursday. The mission was leaving on Friday. I had one day left. My last day.

What would I do?

I couldn't stay home all day. I'd go crazy pacing back and forth, thinking of all the reasons why I should go and the few illogical reasons I should stay. Checking the time, I still had twenty minutes to dress, down some soycakes, and catch the last bus. Sure, I could lie to myself that going to Ridgewood was a good cover and would keep my mind off the mission, but the true reason sat like a rock in my heart. I wanted to see Maxim one more time.

"Jennifer!" Pell shouted from the table as Len dished out the soycakes. "You're feeling better."

"I am." I straightened out my rumpled tunic and took a seat next to her.

"That's wonderful." Len handed me a plate. "How many soycakes do you want?"

"Load it up." Thinking about the dream, I felt like I hadn't eaten anything in years. You're not supposed to eat for a whole twenty-four hours before cryosleep, so I had to pig out now.

Len sat at the table beside Valex. "We're proud of you for getting up today, for going back to school."

I felt like every pore on my face screamed *leaving on a mission to Paradise 15!* I swallowed a mouthful of soycakes and tried to play it calm. "I had to get up sometime. I can't stay in my room all my life."

Pell giggled. "You'd get pretty bored."

I made a goofy face at her. "I'd start eating my socks, like a sock monster."

She laughed so hard that a piece of soycake flew across the table. I thought Valex and Len would be angry, but they laughed. For a moment, we felt like a real family. A family I would leave. In one moment, I saw my life if I stayed on Earth. I'd attend all the events in Pell's life I'd missed in Timmy's—her prom, her graduation, the first day at college, a visit to her new job in the recycling factory, her wedding day.

What would I do with my life? That part of the vision remained fuzzy. I didn't see a place for me in this futuristic world. My heart panged with a sharp pain, and I pushed the thought of the mission from my mind. I needed to enjoy breakfast together one last time.

Pell sat with me on the hoverbus as always, and we talked about her new pink slippers, her math homework, and how Rainy said she looked like one of the pixies on Pixie Swap. When her ride came to an end, she gave me the usual peck on the cheek. I almost burst into tears.

Remember, Jenny, you can't follow Pell around her whole life. You have to have a life of your own. You have to do this for yourself.

Everyone had their place in this world, and mine was on that scout ship. I knew it like I knew my name. That didn't stop the melancholy from dripping in like some old, sour sappy sauce coating my heart.

I got off the hoverbus, and Ridgewood seemed so familiar now, like my old brick high school with trees and Angela and Chad was some useless dream. I scanned the crowd for Maxim. It would be much easier to talk to him without Exara breathing down my neck. A sea of beauties and hunks towered over me, but I couldn't find him in all the pretty faces. My best bet was homeroom. Maybe he was already sitting at his screendesk, waiting for me.

The classroom lay empty besides Mrs. Rickard, who adjusted the brightness of the wallscreen.

"Good morning, Jennifer. It's nice to see you back."

Back from where? My heart jump-started. I hadn't even left yet. Oh, right. I had been out for the last three days.

"Thanks. It's good to be back." I took my seat behind my screendesk.

This was it. The last time I'd see Maxim. I remembered the first day, when my eyes fixated on his perfect features and my heart somersaulted in my chest. I thought someone like that would never even speak to someone like me, and just a few days ago he sat with me on my bed, holding me in his arms. Comforting me from the world. If only I could go back in time.

Now we were as distant as when we first met. Exara would sit in front of me, like some prison guard, and Maxim would pretend nothing had happened between us. Tears brimmed in my eyes.

Why had I come? It would have been much easier to stay home.

The techno jingle rang and students filed in. A backpack dropped by the screendesk in front of me, jarring me out of my trance as I stared at the front door.

"So you finally decided to come back?"

I looked up and Exara's sparkly tunic almost blinded me. She'd curled her auburn hair in perfect ringlets cascading around the curve of her breasts. I wondered how long it took her to get ready for school. I wasn't about to explain the sad turns of my screwed-up life. "Why? Miss me?"

She snorted in disgust. "Just trying to weed out the truth."

"People get sick, don't they?"

"That, or they're afraid to face their mistakes..." She gave me a meaningful stare.

What? Could she have found out about Maxim hugging me on my bed? I gave her a questioning look, and she turned around all smug like she'd just won in a mind game. Great. My last day and I had to deal with her attitude.

Principal Hall's face flashed on the wallscreen and an alarm wailed in my chest. *Wait! Not everyone's here yet.* It can't be time for announcements.

Maxim's screendesk was empty.

To make the morning worse, Exara whirled around and narrowed her icy eyes. "I'll deal with you later."

I stifled a feeling of dread. It took all of my patience to sit through the morning announcements and wait for the techno jingle. Once

Exara strutted off, I approached Mrs. Richardson as she typed on her miniscreen. "Where's Maxim?"

"Maxim Fairweller?" She sighed and patted her fingertip on the touch pad. "He's out for today."

She resumed her typing as if those four words had no meaning to me.

"Out for the day? Why?"

Mrs. Richardson gave me a sly glance. "I'm not allowed to share other students' information."

My heart felt as empty as the room. I'd come to school for Maxim and now I had to suffer through the long day without him. Leaving school early would bring more attention to me, so I had to lie low and pretend life was normal.

The seconds ticked by like hours. Was Maxim okay? Was he sick? Was his family in trouble? Had Exara thrown him out on my account? Or worse—had those mercenaries trying to steal the Timesurfers' technology abducted him to get close to me?

Okay, that last thought was a long shot, but it still flew through my mind, making anxiety eat away at my stomach.

By the time lunch rolled around, I was more likely to chuck my food than digest it. I sat alone in the corner with my lunch container unopened. A little voice inside me said to at least recycle the food so Len wouldn't get suspicious, but I couldn't even bring myself to unlatch the plastic snaps.

Shadows hung around me, and I glanced up. Exara, framed by her lackeys on either side, arrived in a Barbie parade. She stood with both arms crossed, pushing her chest up like two melons below her chin. "What's this I hear about you joining the fencing team, just to steal my boyfriend?"

Oh, that's it? I inwardly sighed with relief. That was *so* last week. For a girl of the future, she was way behind.

I rolled my eyes, trying to look like this Barbie mob didn't bother me. "I'm not trying to steal him."

She pressed her sharp-nailed finger into my chest. The scent of fake bubble gum choked me. "Go find your own guy and stay away from mine."

"Listen, after today, he's all yours."

She pulled her finger away with a shocked look on her face. "Is this some sort of trick?"

I shook my head. "Not at all. You win. You can have him." I looked down at my lunch container. "Just make sure you at least *try* to make him happy."

The techno jingle rang, and everyone bolted from their seats. Her bombshell brigade deserted her for their next classes, and all she could do was get pushed along by the crowd. She stared at me like a dumb princess lost in a foreign land. But I was the one who was lost in the land of *I give up*.

The injustice of her and Maxim left a bitter taste in my mouth, but I couldn't stay around for a thing that wasn't meant to be.

I figured I'd only live in this era once, so I stared right back at her until she tore her gaze away. I had another card to play, but the results wouldn't materialize until I was long gone. I'd have to imagine her face from this memory alone.

The rest of the day I searched for someone who knew where Maxim lived. This was not a conversation I wanted to have on the phone. I needed to talk to him in person. Exara could have him tomorrow, but that left me with the rest of today. After school, I headed toward the cafeteria, remembering today there was a fencing team match.

Shizznizz met me at the door. He'd dyed his hair a bright shade of orange with white strips, reminding me of Nemo. He held his hand across the door, blocking my entrance. "Touché."

I didn't have time for his silly antics. Grabbing his arm, I pulled him aside.

He raised his eyebrows with interest. "I like a woman who's direct."

"Listen, I need to know where Maxim lives."

His face turned serious. "Wait a second, little lady. You need to stay away from that boy. There are plenty of guys around, like *moi*, yours truly here, who are readily available."

I rolled my eyes. Why did everyone think I was a home-wrecker? "I'm not trying to steal him from Exara. I just need to talk to him one last time."

"What? You planning on transferring?" He looked sincerely disappointed, like we could have had something together.

"You could say that." I bit my lip. I couldn't tell him the truth, but he needed something if he was going to tell me where Maxim lived. "I just need to make sure he's all right."

Shizznizz put his hands on his hips. "The boy's been tormented ever since you came to Ridgewood. As one of his best friends, it's my job to make sure he's okay. I can tell you right now, he's just fine."

"Why wasn't he in school today?"

"His little sis had an asthma attack, so he stayed home to look after her. They used to have a real nice robot, a C-9 babysitter edition, but they had to sell it to pay for essentials."

"That's horrible. Will she be okay?"

"She will if you stay the hell away from him. Exara's family is a big whoop-de-doo around here, and if he wants to have a normal life, he won't look a gift horse in the mouth. Sorry, girl, but he shouldn't touch you with a ten-foot samurai blade."

"I talked to Exara, and we're good. I just need to see him one more time."

He gave me a questioning look. "You'll never be good with Exara." A smile curved on his upper lip. "But I won't, either. She's a tough cookie to please."

"Please, Shizz."

"Oh, all right. I'm such a sucker for pretty eyes." He picked up my miniscreen and typed in the coordinates. "This is his high-rise and apartment number. No shenanigans, now. I wouldn't want to have to use this to defend myself." He held up the holster for his laser sword. I pictured Exara going after him, and he'd have no chance. She'd win.

I smiled up at him. A real smile, for a real friend. "Thanks. I owe you one."

"You know it. I won't let you forget it, either."

Turning away, I kept smiling. *Yeah, you can hold it over my cryogenically frozen head.*

CHAPTER THIRTY

Glass Forest

Maxim's high-rise was a lot like Martha's—lingering on the border between sketchy and safe in a part of the city that felt like the middle of nowhere. Paint chipped from the walls, and the hall carpet smelled like old cheese. Couldn't Exara's dad invest in renovations? Or were her beauty treatments too expensive?

Hating her wasn't going to achieve anything, so I threw out my bitter thoughts like old trash and focused on my reasons for visiting.

Why AM I here, anyway? What was I hoping to gain from one last conversation? Resolution? Or did I want him to ask me to stay? If he did, it'd be a tragedy, because the only answer I could give him would be *no*.

I buzzed the door, and Maxim's face flashed on the screen in surprise. I breathed with relief just looking into the pixels that represented his eyes.

"Jenny?"

"Shizznizz gave me your high-rise number." I took a deep breath and calmed my racing heart. "I need to talk to you."

The door panels parted, and he stood in the frame holding a finger to his lips. "Shhhh... Rainy's sleeping."

"Is she okay?" I whispered as I followed him inside. The apartment was small and plain, but tidy. The appliances were older. There were dents in the metal and they had buttons on the keypads, but the interior of the apartment had been repainted, and the air smelled like clean laundry. He wore a simple cotton shirt and dark pants, much like the clothes from my generation. He must have saved the fancy tunics for school. I wondered how such a hot guy could come from such a dismal place.

"She'll be fine. These kinds of things happen all the time. Usually one of my parents is able to stay home with her, but they found jobs at the soybean factory and work all sorts of hours for a small amount of what my dad used to earn alone."

"I'm sorry." I wanted to promise him that I'd make sure no one in his family ever had to work again, but that comment would give me away. I couldn't let him know where I was going. He might try to stop me.

Maxim shrugged. "It's life." He gestured toward the couch. "Want to sit down?"

"Sure." Suddenly I had nothing left to say. I wanted to be here with him, but anything I said would only lead me to places I couldn't go. I felt like a ballet dancer with no legs, a bird with no wings.

"I needed to talk to you, too." Maxim sat beside me, so close our legs touched.

My heart pounded. "Why?"

"I got some strange calls today from Exara and Shizz. Exara said you talked like you were going to die or something, and Shizz said you were transferring schools." He took my hand and cradled it in both of his. "What's going on?"

Stupid Exara has to ruin everything. Tears blurred my eyes. "I'm not supposed to say."

"It's something with the Timesurfers, isn't it?"

"If I tell you anything, I'll put you in danger. You'll become an accomplice, and you can't afford to get into trouble. Not with Rainy in the state she's…"

"Tell me one thing." Maxim leaned in, his forehead resting on mine. "Will I see you again?"

I closed my eyes and shook my head. He could interpret it as though I couldn't tell him, or as the truth.

Warm lips pressed against mine, and my eyes shot open as he kissed me. I opened my lips slightly and kissed him back, running my tongue over his perfect teeth. His hand traveled up my back to my neck, and he drew me in further, pulling me against him with need. I tangled my fingers through his hair like all the times I'd imagined in my dreams, but this was better than anything I could have invented. We fell back on the couch, me on top of him, our bodies melting into one another.

My brain shut off, and desire took over. I ran my hands up and down his body, feeling every inch of him, wanting to be closer still. He reacted like my touch was magic, kissing me deeper as my hands slid underneath his shirt.

Must. Come. Off.

I tugged at the buttons as he placed kisses down my neck and whispered my name softly, making my skin tingle. His chest was hard and smooth, and I longed to rub my bare skin over it. He pulled up the sides of my tunic, his hands traveling over the curves of my body, lighting me on fire.

A faint beeping sound stole my attention. Maxim surfaced from a kiss and his eyes opened wide. "It's Rainy. I have to check on her."

I slid off him, feeling the cool air where his body had been.

Maxim disappeared into her room.

I stood up and inched toward her bedroom door.

"Are you all right?" Maxim's voice shook with worry.

"Yeah, I just need a glass of water." It was the first time I'd heard Rainy speak. Her voice was soft and sweet, like a fuzzy animal in a cartoon.

"Here you go, Pixiehead."

She laughed lightly, and I knew she was all right. Then reality came barging in like a semi through a forest of glass. I was leaving tomorrow for Paradise 15. Anything I did today with Maxim would only complicate our lives, only hold us both back. He needed to follow his dreams, and I needed to follow mine. They just didn't intersect like in fairy tales.

I shouldn't be here.

Maxim would come out any minute. Before I could change my mind, I collected my things and headed for the door. Thankfully, the panels parted silently, and I bolted down the hall toward the hoverbus platform. Each step felt like I was ripping my heart open more, but I forced myself to keep running. There was a bus ready to take off, and I waved it down with tears streaking my cheeks.

The operator gave me an annoyed grimace as I jumped on. "Gonna make me late for the next stop."

"Sorry, sir." I took a seat in the first row.

Then I heard my name. The voice was muted, from outside.

Maxim stood on the platform, but he was too late.

I placed my hot hand on the cool glass and watched him grow smaller as the hoverbus sped away.

CHAPTER THIRTY-ONE

Clearance

I scanned my room, glancing over everything I owned. So little, and none of it felt like mine. I'd lost all my real belongings when I was frozen before. These items were just meager substitutes, and I didn't mind leaving most of them behind.

Packing took my mind off Maxim. I focused my efforts on bringing only useful items for the mission. Warm clothes came first, followed by comfortable walking boots. I glanced at the videos as if my parents called my name through the shiny surface. Although they were the only link to my past, I doubted Paradise 15 would have a DVD player. I didn't have time for Valex to transfer the data, and any request like that would alert him of my plan. Instead, I shoved in the album Valex and Len had given me. It took up a lot of space, and I couldn't use it for anything practical, but it held pictures of everyone dear to me. Everyone except Maxim.

I ran my tongue over my lips, thinking about the feeling of his mouth on mine. My heart raced when I thought of lying on top of him, of how he reacted to my touch.

Maybe not having a picture of Maxim was a *good* thing.

I threw in my favorite hairbrush, a pack of soywafers, and my pocketknife. I dug through my drawer. Maxim's card. The one he gave me that first day at lunch. I hovered over the recycling chute. It was the only thing I had to remind me of him. *Just throw it away.*

Instead, I slid it in the backpack under the cover of the album. I knew I couldn't call him from deep space from my frozen cryotube, but it didn't weigh much or take up additional space. What harm would it cause to take it? I could always throw it away later…or keep it forever on a cord dangling from my neck.

I was such a hopeless romantic.

Thursday night passed achingly slowly. The fluorescent numbers seemed to take forever to change on the wallscreen and I braided my hair into a thousand tiny braids and unbraided it, over and over again. My hair looked like I'd crimped it with a hot iron, but I had to keep my fingers busy while my mind ran in circles.

The next morning, I waited until everyone left before exiting my room. Len had knocked on the door twice, but I told her I needed more sleep. If any of them had seen my face, it would have given me away. Besides, it was easier if I didn't have to say good-bye, if I pretended I was heading out for the day and would return after school.

I loaded the letter I'd already written to them on my wallscreen. By the time they found it, I'd be taking off on the ship, already frozen. Besides, they couldn't stop me. I was eighteen, and it was my choice. I could only hope they'd come to accept my decision in time. What I was leaving behind for them would, hopefully, soften the burden.

C-7 dusted the shelves in the living room as I walked toward the door. "Good morning, Jennifer. If I must say, you are quite a bit late for school."

"I'm not going to school today, C-7."

He stopped dusting, his silver fingers hovering over the shelf. "Is it time?"

My eyes burned with unshed tears. "Yes. I'm going away with the Timesurfers. I'm going to follow my dreams."

C-7 dropped the cloth on the floor and walked over. "May you find what you are looking for."

Stick to business, Jenny, or you'll lose it. "Listen, I don't want to get you into trouble. I left a note for Valex, Len, and Pell on my wallscreen. They'll know this is my decision alone."

"Do not worry about me. Life will go on as planned."

I stepped toward him and held out my hand. The very first day I hadn't wanted to touch him, but now I needed to reach out. He'd done so much for me. "Thank you for helping me."

AUBRIE DIONNE

His silver fingers closed over mine. "It was my pleasure. Thank you for being my friend."

I smiled, feeling way more emotional than I should. To me, C-7 was like a person, not some household appliance. "Give it some time with Pell. I know she'll come around."

C-7's mouth snapped shut as if he didn't agree. He shook his head, gears buzzing. "It took bringing someone back from a lost generation to truly understand."

I couldn't stay with him forever and, as much as I wanted to take him with me, I couldn't steal Valex and Len's robot. "You do a fine job for this family. Take care of them for me."

C-7 nodded, the plates bending in his slender neck. "I will."

Not looking back, I left the apartment where I'd spent most of my time in this futuristic world. I jogged to the platform and waited for the hoverbus, checking my miniscreen every minute as the time grew closer to eleven-twenty-one. A black hovercraft pulled up right on the money, and the hatch opened like the gate to my destiny.

Maybe I was being overly dramatic.

My hair fanned out around me as I stepped on the ramp. The hovercraft hummed so loud it rumbled in my gut, but at least it had panels to block the rush of air buoying it up. Yara's slender face poked out from the shadows. She wore a black jumpsuit, much like Jax's. Would I get one, too? *I'll probably look more like a janitor than a ninja.*

Yara gave me a sour curve of her lips and nodded her head in acknowledgment. "Jennifer."

"Nice to see you, too."

Figured she'd be the one to pick me up. I settled into a seat in back where I couldn't see out the sight panel, then folded my hands in my lap. Would I miss this high-rise world? Only time would tell. The adrenaline coursing through my veins burned away the melancholy, and all I could do was think about Paradise 15. The next time I woke up, I'd be on standing on a new planet, getting ready to bring animals back to life. I had been willing to travel to the ends of the earth to save creatures that couldn't save themselves, and now I'd travel to the ends of the galaxy. The stakes were higher, and it only made me crave adventure even more.

We drove for so long that I unbelted myself to check the sight panel. The wall surrounding the city came up, patrolled by government troops with laser guns and hovercrafts.

"Where are we going?"

Yara sneered. "You didn't think we'd take off from underground, did you?"

Actually, I hadn't thought about it. A spaceship needed a launchpad and tons of room. Where would we find that in a land crammed with high-rises?

"Will they let us through?"

"They should. We have the correct codes. It's easier to leave the city than to get back in." Yara's voice was steady, but her fingers tightened on the railing, knuckles turning white.

The wall rose up so high and so thick I couldn't see past it. "What's on the other side?"

"More high-rises for miles, then the barrens—land that's been farmed to dust. It's a wasteland. Nothing survives."

As our hovercraft approached, the men raised their lasers in our direction.

The pilot must have handled the exchange, because Yara and I stood frozen, watching the hovercrafts buzz around us like giant wasps.

I whispered, as if they could hear me through the thick glass, "Do they know who we are?"

"No. We're under the guise of civilians visiting family outside the city."

"What's the difference between being on this side or that?"

Yara sighed as if she had to explain the world to a two-year-old.

I was annoyed, but my curiosity won over and I waited for her to get over herself. "Well?"

"There are more greenhouses here, more food."

"Those poor people." Casting a glance at my backpack, I suddenly felt like I should have packed more soybean wafers. Why didn't they teach me important survival stuff like this at Ridgewood? Instead, I spent all those hours recalculating Einstein's equations and drawing light bursts on my miniscreen.

"Don't worry. Our base is equipped with everything we will need. Besides, we won't be there for very long."

The guards brought their guns down, and the hovercraft sped forward. Yara's face softened as we held on to the railing to avoid falling back. "We got clearance."

Outside the wall, the high-rises stretched on for another thirty minutes, like too many pencils shoved in a jar, each one capped with a greenhouse. Most of those glass tops looked empty; the only plants I could see appeared to be shriveled brown or dead. As we drove farther from the city, the buildings shrank below us. At first I thought we flew higher in the sky, but the structures weren't as tall. Some of them almost looked like skyscrapers from my time.

The buildings grew farther apart, too. Wide alleys stretched in between them, filled with garbage and heaps of sandy dirt. The spaces grew until only small shacks appeared on a dusty-brown landscape. It could have been the great Sahara. "Where are all the buildings?"

Yara raised her voice to be heard over the hum of the engines. "Since you've been frozen, Earth's climate has grown violent and unpredictable. Terrible hurricanes down south, volcanos erupting on the Hawaiian Islands, tsunamis on the West Coast, dust storms in the nation's interior."

Now I saw why we needed a new planet. "The world's gone to hell."

Yara snorted. "Leave it to people to ruin the world."

Who'd run Paradise 15? The animals? Yara? Tightening my lips, I decided not to comment.

The hovercraft's engines rumbled below my feet, and we descended to a patch of flat, dry dirt. "We're in the middle of nowhere."

Standing up, Yara laughed like I was an idiot. "That's what we want you to think."

CHAPTER THIRTY-TWO

Legacy

The hatch opened, and I covered my mouth with my sleeve as a blast of sand stung my skin. I followed Yara down the ramp, covering my eyes from the searing gusts that seemed to want to rip me into pieces. After the wind died, I glanced up at two adobe buildings the same color as the sand. Invisible from the sky, they stretched out, low to the ground. Yara led me to the first one and we stumbled in through a glass doorway. Only after the doors sealed behind me could I breathe again.

A woman with dark curly hair looked up from a gray plastic desk, regarding us like we had just walked in from off the street. "Can I help you?"

Yara ran her fingers through her hair. Sand particles sprinkled onto the dark green carpet. "We're here to see Doctor Sparks."

She sipped from an overly large coffee mug. "I'll buzz him."

While we waited for the doctor, the hovercraft took off. We really *were* stranded in the middle of nowhere. All those visions I had had of my family or Maxim running to stop me were put to rest. There was no way any of them could get to me in time to change my mind. That thought made me melancholy but gave me an exhilarating kind of freedom.

A bearded man, framed by scientists in white lab coats, entered the lobby. The scientists gave me a questioning look as I passed, reminding me of the cold eyes in my dream. I shrugged it off and stared back at them with pride.

"Doctor Sparks." Yara shook his hand and smiled with familiarity. He acknowledged Yara with a nod. "Is this her?"

"Yes." Yara dusted off her shoulders. "Jennifer Streetwater, final member of team Centauri Beta."

"Excellent. You're right on time."

The scientists led us into separate rooms. My room looked like a doctor's office, with strange medical equipment hanging from the walls and a white, sheet-less bed in the center. Panic rose up in my throat. Had I been tricked?

"Remove your civilian clothes and wear this." Dr. Sparks handed me a black ninja suit like Jax's and left, along with the rest of the scientists.

Holding the suit to my chest, I thought of Jax, and my racing heart calmed. He wouldn't trick me into anything. Checking for hidden cameras, I slipped off the tunic Valex and Len had given me. I couldn't fit it in my backpack, so I'd have to leave it behind. The fabric clumped on the floor and I felt like I'd rejected their goodwill. *I hope they forgive me.* I also felt as though I was breaking free of a fake persona—Jennifer the future girl. I wasn't meant for this over-populated, high-rise world.

I stepped into the uniform and zipped the front all the way up to my neck. A starship flying over a green planet was embroidered on the right breast. The symbol of the Timesurfers? I ran my fingers over the rough patterns of the helm against the blackness of deep space. *That will be me.* It did look pretty cool.

A middle-aged woman with gray hair tied in a tight bun came in. Although she wore the same blank white lab coat as the other scientists, her eyes were warm. "Hello, dear. I'm here to take your vital signs." She checked my eyes, ears, and blood pressure. All normal things. I was thankful for her gentle nature. Jumpy as I was, anyone else would have made me scream.

She held a beeping device up to my face and a blue light flashed in my eyes. "Let me explain the cryogenic procedure—"

"Don't." I blinked away the blue flash of light. "I've already been through it once. I don't need to be reminded again."

"Okay, dear. You know you need to sign this disclaimer..."

She handed me a screen stating the possible side effects of cryogenic sleep. I couldn't recall ever signing something like this before, but then again, I was underage last time. My parents probably signed it for me.

I took the plastic pen and squiggled my name over the screen. My signature never looked the way I wanted it to.

"You are aware it's illegal to freeze anyone deemed healthy, correct?" The nurse gave me a meaningful stare.

I shook my head. "I had no idea. Why?"

"The survival rate is fifty-three percent. It's not high enough for the government to endorse it. Some see it as suicide, others as a crazy recreational activity—living longer to see what will become of the world. Surfing through time, if you will."

"So that's why they picked me. I've lived through it before."

She scanned me with some handheld machine and checked the readings. "That's one of the reasons. Yes, hon. You have proved to be especially hardy."

She smiled as if I'd just won a prize in a talent show. Then, in another heartbeat, her face hardened back into a serious frown. "For us to freeze you, we have to tamper with your records, make you look like you've been sick."

She clicked on the screen and handed it back to me. "You'll need to sign a document stating you're okay with this."

Signing a disclosure form seemed superfluous considering they could all be arrested for illegal activities. But if I wanted to be on this mission, I had to follow orders. I glanced at the screen, feeling I was exposing myself to some form of cruel punishment. *This is for Thunderbolt and all those animals driven to extinction.*

I closed my eyes, took a deep breath, and signed my name. When I handed the screen back to her, I felt I'd already accomplished something. I'd faced my fears.

"Come now. You have a meeting with a lawyer to ensure the survival of your estate and settle any unresolved debts."

I followed her into a meeting room with a large desk, the plastic made to resemble rich wood. It reminded me of my dad's. An elderly man with wispy white hair, dressed in a tunic suit, shook my hand. "Nice to meet you, Jennifer. My name is Reddic Halefern, and I'm here to discuss how you'd like to leave your estate. You have quite an estate to dictate, Ms. Streetwater. Please, have a seat."

I'd been planning for this ever since I heard Jax's message saying I was on the team. I'd researched my bank account with the help of C-7. I knew exactly how much was in there. Plopping into a cushy chair, I crossed my legs. This would take some time.

"First of all, I'd like to leave thirty million credits to Maxim Fairweller. Enough to ensure the well-being of his entire family and especially his younger sister, Rainy."

Reddic Halefern raised an eyebrow and began to type. "Very well."

"Make sure he can't refuse the gift. I'd like the following message attached."

Mr. Halefern glanced at me. "Go ahead."

I shifted in my seat and the plastic cushion creaked under my butt. I felt weird saying such personal things to this elderly man whom I'd never met, but I had something I had to say. "Tell him, 'Now you're free to follow your dreams.'"

He nodded, and it took me a few moments to swallow my raging emotions before I could speak again. In a way, telling Maxim to follow his dreams was a way of letting him go.

I counted on my fingers to make sure I didn't leave anyone out. "Next, I'd like to leave fifty million credits to my legal guardians, Valex and Len Streetwater, and twenty million to their daughter, Pell." It wasn't that I didn't believe in Pell. She definitely could make it on her own in this competitive high-rise world, but having a little buffer couldn't hurt.

He continued to type. "It will be done."

The old man pressed a few keys and looked over the screen. "Anything else?"

"Yes. Martha Maynard needs a new cat."

Mr. Halefern's eyebrows rose and he leaned his head to the right, as if he hadn't heard me correctly.

"We both work for the Timesurfers... If they could replicate a freaking horse and jungle monkeys, you'd think the least they could do for an old lady is a kitten. I'm willing to pay whatever it takes."

He scratched his chin. "It is an odd request, but doable, yes."

I sat up, beaming like Santa Claus the day after Christmas. "Good. Make sure she gets the new kitten as soon as possible."

"The process should take two to three months."

"Good. Tell her it's a new friend for Jumbo."

Mr. Halefern nodded and continued to type.

I considered giving Martha a nicer apartment, but somehow I knew deep down she wouldn't move. Old people got so stuck in their ways. The least I could do was make sure she'd have enough to live on for the rest of her life. "And give her ten million credits. Tell her to do with it as she sees fit."

"Consider it done."

I swiveled in the chair, feeling I could finally do some good in the world.

He wrinkled his hairy gray eyebrows. "What about the rest of your estate?"

"Give all but ten million to the Timesurfers, and have the rest invested for future use." Who knew? After all, I *was* planning to come back in another five hundred years to claim it.

"Very well, Ms. Streetwater."

I stood up, feeling overly sentimental and generous, like Ebenezer Scrooge after the three ghosts came to visit him. "One more thing. Give yourself a million credits."

"Ms. Streetwater?"

I winked. "It's a tip. To make sure my wishes are carried out."

Mr. Halefern rose up from his desk and bowed like a butler in a fairy tale. "I will see to it personally."

CHAPTER THIRTY-THREE

Centauri Beta

I left the meeting with the lawyer on cloud nine, tingling happiness spreading throughout my body. Everyone I knew would be taken care of. I was free to do this mission with a clear conscience and devote my heart and soul to the success of the Timesurfers on Paradise 15.

The woman from the front desk led me into a waiting room where other members of the team awaited further orders. As I walked in, Yara muttered under her breath. Jax stood in the center in his black ninja uniform.

He caught my eyes and jogged to meet me. His usually spiked hair was slicked back, bringing out the strong bone structure of his face, his sparkling blue eyes, and his boyishly round nose. He wrapped his arms around me and picked me up, twirling in a circle before putting me down again. *Yara didn't get this kind of greeting.*

"Jennifer! I'm so glad you decided to join us." He looked me up and down. "You look stunning in our uniform."

I glanced at my boots, trying to hide the heat in my cheeks. "I'm pumped to be here."

"Everything is running smoothly. Now that you're here, we can walk to the launching platform. First, I'd like you to meet the other members of the team."

He waved two men over. One of them looked just a few years older than us, with a lanky frame and curly blond hair. The other guy had gray streaks running through his dark hair. He must have just made the age-limit cut.

The young man shook my hand first.

Jax cut in, "This is Theo Woodward. He's our medical officer. Theo, meet Jennifer Streetwater, our animal specialist."

Theo shook my hand and smiled warmly. "Nice to meet you."

"Same here." His hair reminded me of Timmy's, and I blocked the reference out, turning to the other man. His hand was big and burly, but he shook my hand gently.

"Terrance Williams, mechanic."

Because their names were all normal-sounding, I wondered if they'd all been frozen like Jax and me, but now wasn't the time to get personal. Jax had assured me he'd done tests for compatibility to make sure we'd work well together.

"And you know Yara, our botanist."

After Jax's flamboyant display of attention, I was afraid to even turn my head in her direction. "Yeah."

Either Jax ignored my obvious lack of enthusiasm, or he was too excited to see it. "Fantastic. Let's go see the ship, shall we?"

Jax led us down a long plastic tube that connected the building to the platform. The desert stretched out in either direction in an endless slate of desolation. The plastic quivered in the raging wind as we walked, and I was afraid it would rip the tube in half and we'd all go flying into the dust.

Audible gasps rang out. I glanced up. A dark shape cast a dark shadow ahead of us, partially obscured by the opacity of the plastic tunnel. It was long and tall like a rocket ship. Two round engines flanked the ship on either side.

We reached a part of the tunnel where a glass door led out to the platform. The silver hull shone in a polished gleam, defying the sand with its smooth, impenetrable surface. I had to bend my head all the way back to see the pointed tip against the sun. The Timesurfers' symbol of a starship over a planet was painted on the side, along with the number 8573 in black. It was magnificent, daunting, and exciting all at the same time. My whole body shivered in awe.

This was my destiny. The certainty of my fate washed over me, and I couldn't imagine being anywhere else.

"A quick sprint and we're there." Jax smiled as he placed his hand on the door. "The sandstorms quiet down later in the day, so we should be safe. Everyone ready?"

"Ready to roll." Theo clapped his hands and rubbed them together. Beside him, Yara nodded, followed by Terrance. Jax cast me a look of expectation and I nodded.

I can do this.

The doors parted and we ran to the platform. I squinted through the sand to keep track of the others. Jax climbed up metal ladder rings cemented into the platform's side, and we each followed. As I climbed, I focused on putting one hand over the other, trying not to breathe through my mouth or the sand would come flying in. My stomach gurgled, and I longed for my soywafers, but we weren't supposed to eat anything before being frozen. Why had I even brought them? They wouldn't last through hundreds of years. Gritting my teeth, I ignored the hunger pains. *I'll be sleeping soon enough, and then I won't feel anything.* Or at least I hoped I wouldn't.

We passed by scientists dressed in full bodysuits, with plastic shielding their faces, taking readings on the ship. Jax ran underneath the belly to a ramp leading inside. I followed him and the rest of the team. Wiping sand from my eyes, I stood in a loading bay with two giant trucks, reminding me of Hummers on steroids, on either side. The tires alone were taller than me, with giant grooves and spikes on either side.

Jax waved his hands. "Junglerovers. Our transports once we land. Terrance has been learning how to drive them out here in the desert."

Terrance chuckled. "Piece of cake."

"Great. I'll take you on a tour, and then we're off to the cryolab on the main deck."

Cryolab. I pushed down the memory of my dream and followed Jax as he buzzed an elevator.

We emerged on a floor with a series of rooms, all sealed by thick metal doors. "These are our supplies." Jax pressed a code into a panel and the doors to the first room parted to reveal boxes stacked to the ceiling. "Food, water, extra clothes. It will all be frozen along with us to prevent any decay. Oh, that reminds me." He gestured for all of us to come closer. "You'll need to take off your backpacks and leave them in here. That way your belongings will be preserved as well."

Maybe I'd eat those soywafers after all. Following the others, I leaned my backpack up against the supply containers. Jax secured the packs with a bungee cord and resealed the room. "On to the computer mainframe."

He took us up another level, which spread out into one giant deck. Wallscreens lined the walls. Wires ran down through the floor and up above our heads like a nest of snakes.

Jax turned on a screen. There was a countdown to takeoff. My heart skipped a beat.

"The ground scientists are going to remote-activate this ship and drive it through the atmosphere into deep space. Once our trajectory is chosen, the computer will take over."

What happened if the computer messed up? I opened my mouth to protest, but thought better of it. Hours before takeoff wasn't the appropriate time to voice concerns. Instead, I ran my fingers along a clump of wires, feeling the sturdiness of the plastic coating. Computers didn't make mistakes, did they?

Jax must have seen fear in my face. "This would never work with a giant colony transport ship. Too many systems to keep online, but a simple scout ship like this will be fine."

Theo chimed in, "So who wakes us up?"

Jax led us out of the room. "Our cryotubes are programmed to wake us up once we reach Paradise 15."

If I ever was afraid I wouldn't wake up, now was the time. This whole mission seemed sketchier than the first time I was frozen. At least then I was still on Earth in a hospital with doctors all around to monitor my status. The craziest part was, I was determined to go, whether it scared the heebie-jeebies out of me or not.

CHAPTER THIRTY-FOUR

Final Thoughts

The cryolab sat before us like the mouth to the underworld. I kept eyeing it nervously as Jax spoke about the ship's navigational systems. It was like sitting in front of the toilet and waiting to hurl. You knew it would be scary and gross, but you had to do it in order to feel better.

Jax turned toward me. "That's how we'll avoid running into nebulas or comets…"

I gulped down my fear. I tried to give him a reassuring smile, but my stomach twisted in knots.

"Jennifer, you okay?" Jax put a hand on my shoulder.

Yara scoffed beside us, like I was playing sick *on purpose* to get his attention.

I ignored her and held my arms around my stomach. "Yes, I'm just feeling a little queasy."

Jax looked at everyone behind me. "Why don't the rest of you go to the cryolab and get ready? Jennifer and I'll join you shortly."

Theo and Terrance took off with a few grunts, and Yara made sure to fire her laser eyes at me before she turned away. I turned to Jax, my chin trembling. I hated myself for letting fear get the better of me.

Jax cupped my chin in his hand. "Talk to me—what's wrong?"

A thousand doubts ran through my mind. "What if we don't wake up? Or what if I'm the *only* one who wakes up? What if the computer wakes us up at the wrong time, or—"

Jax put a finger to my lips. "We've both done this before. I'll be right beside you the entire trip. When you wake up, I swear on my daughter's grave, I'll be there by your side."

I blinked back tears. "There are some things even you can't control."

"I have a good feeling about this. We can do this, you and I. We can save those animals and live in a society without high-rises, sprawling green land on all sides."

His dreams were mine. The only difference was that he had the conviction to override the fear.

Jax held my face in both his hands. Tears rimmed his eyes. "I'm not going to force you to do anything. You can still go back."

I thought of flying in a hovercraft back into the city, returning home to Valex, Len and Pell, seeing Maxim again. I'd still be stuck in a world where I didn't belong. I'd be a nobody. This was the chance for me to be a true hero.

"No." I put my hands over Jax's and brought his hands down from my face. "I want to go."

He looked like relief had splashed him in the face. Laughing, he leaned over and kissed my forehead. When he pulled back, his eyes were so intense.

Wonder if he thought of kissing me anywhere else.

He took a deep breath, looking at me like I was his salvation. "Then what are we waiting for?"

I followed Jax into the cryolab with so many emotions running through me that my head felt like a thunderstorm. Jax had feelings for me—it was in his eyes. The idea was so new to me; I had no idea how to feel about it, and there was no more time to think.

Nurses lowered me into my cryotube and hooked me up. I couldn't see Jax's face, but I knew his tube was next to mine, as promised. I wished I could stick my arm out through the side and hold his hand. Instead, my arms were laid on either side of me. My breathing grew heavy, and the nurse instructed me to count down from ten.

10 What if I have feelings for Jax?
9 Wouldn't it just get in the way of our mission?
8 I wonder what Paradise 15 will look like.

7 Will Valex and Len forgive me?
6 I hope Pell succeeds in life.
5 Everything is getting cold.
4 Will our mission be a success?
3 Would my parents be proud?
2 Will Maxim come after me?
1

The End

Acknowledgments

FIRSTLY, I'D LIKE TO THANK KATE KAYNAK AND EVERYONE AT SPENCER HILL PRESS FOR TAKING ON SUCH A STRANGE AND UNIQUE BOOK. I have wonderful editors to thank as well: Rich Storrs and Vikki Ciaffone, who found new ways to develop the story to its full potential. I'd like to thank my publicist, Damaris, for supporting me well before this book was even out there. Next comes my agent, Dawn Dowdle, for her patient wisdom. My sister, Brianne, deserves deep thanks for buying all my books on her Kindle even though she's already read them. Next, my parents, Joanne and Andy, for their love and support. My flute teacher and life mentor, Peggy Vagts, for believing in me with both my careers. Lastly, my husband, Chris.

About the Author

AUBRIE DIONNE IS AN AUTHOR AND FLUTIST IN NEW ENGLAND. Her books have been highly rated by Romance Times Magazine, as well as Night Owl Reviews and Two Lips Reviews. She has guest-blogged on the USA Today *Happily Ever After Blog* and the *Dear Teen Me* blog and signed books at the Boston Book Festival and the Romance Writers of America conference. Her books are published by Entangled Publishing, Harper Impulse, Astraea Press, Spencer Hill Press, Inkspell Publishing, and Lyrical Press.

CPSIA information can be obtained at www.ICGtesting.com
Printed in the USA
LVOW10s1356141114

413714LV00006B/6/P